I0657286

Hermann Otto Nietschmann, Emma A. Endlich

Katharine von Bora- Dr. Martin Luthers Wife

A picture from life

Hermann Otto Nietschmann, Emma A. Endlich

Katharine von Bora- Dr. Martin Luthers Wife
A picture from life

ISBN/EAN: 9783743427228

Printed in Europe, USA, Canada, Australia, Japan

Cover: Foto ©Raphael Reischuk / pixelio.de

Manufactured and distributed by brebook publishing software (www.brebook.com)

Hermann Otto Nietschmann, Emma A. Endlich

Katharine von Bora- Dr. Martin Luthers Wife

KATHARINE VON BORA,

Dr. Martin Luther's Wife.

A PICTURE FROM LIFE,

BY

ARMIN STEIN.

TRANSLATED BY E. A. ENDLICH.

PHILADELPHIA:

G. W. FREDERICK,

1890.

AUTHOR'S PREFACE.

IT has been my purpose in "Katharine von Bora," to picture in the peaceful quiet of his domestic happiness, the man whose influence so largely shaped the course of public events.

The undertaking has not been altogether an easy one; for, while history flows in a copious stream, regarding the Reformer himself, it gives but meager information as to the great man's wife,—the humble, modest woman, who never thrust herself forward, nor sought any personal advantage from her husband's greatness,—but remained contentedly in the background, glad to do him service, and to enrich her own heart from the abundance of his spiritual riches. Only occasional fragments give us glimpses of Katharine's life, and out of these I will endeavor to form a completer picture.

The fact that Luther is so absorbing a personality, gives rise to a further difficulty,—the biography of Katharine von Bora often insensibly becomes that of

3

Luther himself; and the author pauses to ask himself: Am I writing of Katharine, or of Luther? I can only repeat, that it is my purpose, in this book, to paint Luther's domestic life, and therefore Dr. Martin, as the head of his household, may fitly play a leading part.

As has already been stated, the historical notices regarding Katharine von Bora are very scant. In addition to the laborious compilation by Walsh, published in refutation of popish calumnies, there are but two learned works upon the subject,—Hofman's " Katharine von Bora ; or, Luther as Husband and Father," and a ·'Life of Katharine von Bora," by W. Beste ; besides these, I would mention a concise and popular sketch, written by Meurer, the Luther-biographer.

It has been my endeavor, so to utilize the material here gathered, that our people may learn to know the wife of its greatest man,—not by name only, but as her husband's " helpmeet," in the truest sense of the word, as a pattern of domestic virtue, and as a pearl among women.

CONTENTS.

5

BOOK SECOND—THE WIFE.

CHAPTER XXI.

CHAPTER XXII.

CHAPTER XXIII.

CHAPTER XXIV.

BOOK THIRD—THE WIDOW.

CHAPTER XXV.

CHAPTER XXVI.

CHAPTER XXVII.

CHAPTER XXVIII.

CHAPTER XXIX.

KATHARINE VON BORA;

THE MAIDEN.

———•———

CHAPTER I.

A CONSPIRACY.

IT was the evening of a clear, warm March day. The sun, sinking behind the distant hills, sent its parting rays over the earth, tinting hills and valleys, forests and meadows, with golden light. The evening mist was rising, and covering with a filmy veil the tender spring flowers—the snow-drops and violets—from the chilly night air. The windows in the western wing of the convent of Nimptschen shone with a ruddy glow; and the face of the young nun, who stood by an open casement, seemed transfigured by the strange light, while the tears in her eyes quivered like drops of liquid gold. With longing sadness, her glance rested upon the landscape; upon the peasants, returning to their homes, after the day's work; and upon the children, playing their merry games on the village green. The young nun was of pleasing, grace-

(9)

ful figure.   Her features were too irregular to be strictly beautiful, and the pallor of her skin made her appear older than she was.   But her face possessed the
rare charm of sympathy.   Clear, thoughtful eyes and
delicately curved lips betrayed a deep, rich inner life,
and a sensitive heart; while the firmly rounded chin
bespoke self-respect and decision of character.   An
expression of gentle dignity lay upon the arched forehead.   There was in her manner a certain highbred
nobility, the stamp of true womanliness, and her
movements were full of grace.

Her cell was narrow and gloomy; yet the skillful
hands of its occupant had so disposed the scanty furniture, and the saints' pictures upon the walls, adding
here and there little touches of color, that the room
had lost its bare appearance.   The abbess herself was
fond of visiting this cell, and often said: "I cannot
understand, Sister Katharine, why your cell is so home-
like.   One feels here, that it is far pleasanter to come,
than to go."

As the nun stood by the window, her tearful eyes
rested upon the calm beauty of the early Springtime,
while her mind was lost in gloomy reveries.   At her
feet lay a piece of costly violet-colored velvet, which
had dropped from her hands, and upon the window
ledge were tangled masses of white and yellow silk.

Rousing herself from her dreams, she hastily gathered up the velvet, sat down upon a stool, and resumed her embroidery. It was an altar-cloth for the convent-church. The design was, two palm branches crossed, and above, the legend "Ave Maria." The words were already finished; but the branches were merely outlined in coarse stitches. Her slender fingers moved wearily over the velvet, and her head bent low over her work, for the last scant rays of daylight were falling into the cell.

Suddenly, the heavy, iron-mounted door was opened, and a younger nun appeared. "What is this, Sister Katharine?" she exclaimed, in surprise. "Still at your work? Pray spare your eyes! But," she continued, coming nearer, "why are you so far behindhand? What will the abbess say? To-morrow, at High Mass, the altar was to wear its new draperies."

Katharine looked up with a dreary smile. "I am angry with my own heart, because it is so reluctant to obey the commands of our Superior. My needle moves slowly; and what was once a pleasure, has become a burden. O Sister Elizabeth, a change has come over my soul, since the voice of the Monk of Wittenberg penetrated these walls!"

Elizabeth glanced anxiously toward the door.

"Speak softly, Sister Katharine, these walls have ears." She pushed the bolt, and drawing a stool beside Katharine, she sat down, saying gently: "Light the lamp, Sister, I will help you."

"How kind you are, dear Elizabeth," exclaimed Katharine, with a grateful smile. "But let us wait— it is time for vespers."

As she spoke, the little bell was heard, summoning the nuns to evening prayers. Then followed the meagre supper in the refectory.

Both nuns were of noble lineage, for the Cistercian Convent Marienthron at Nimptschen received no others. The younger one was Elizabeth von Kanitz, who had taken the veil but a year and a half ago. Her fresh, rose-tinted skin had not yet been blanched by the cellar-like atmosphere of the convent, nor her cheerful spirit crushed by the oppressive discipline of the order. Her ingenuous, childlike disposition had won the love of the Sisters, and even the venerable abbess had been seen to smile at her merry sallies. Her friend was a descendant of the distinguished family Von Bora, richer in noble ancestors than in worldly goods. She was an orphan, and knew but one member of her family to be living, her brother, Hans von Bora. She had reached her twenty-fourth year, and had been in the convent since her childhood, having taken the final vows at the age of fifteen.

An hour later, we find them again in Katharine's cell. The copper lamp was lighted, and they sat down together, to finish the embroidery which was to be used at the celebration on the morrow.

"How swiftly your finger fly, dear Elizabeth," said Katharine, "and how contentedly your eyes rest upon your work. You happy child ! Life is all a fair May-day to you ! Doubts and temptations are all unknown to you. You are satisfied within these gloomy walls, and to your childlike faith they seem to lead straight to heaven. I, too, was once happy and contented here, although I grieved sorely at leaving my father's house. Ah, it is hard, to part forever from all that is dear to us, and to hear the convent gates close behind us, like the lid of a coffin ; to be dead to the outer world ; never again to receive the kiss of love, or the greeting of friendship. But seeing that it must needs be,—for my parents, with their small means, could not provide a suitable refuge for their daughter, I overcame my sorrow, and with confident hope knocked at these doors, of which I was told that they were the doors of Heaven. And truly, it seemed as though a breath from Heaven greeted me, as I crossed the threshold. To be sheltered from the temptations of an evil world, and from the cares of this life ; to

be surrounded by the odor of incense, and the sound
of holy music; to be guided at every step by spiritual
counsel; to be able to labor unceasingly for the welfare of my soul, and fix my thoughts upon the life to
come,—all this persuaded me that I had entered the
courts of Heaven, and I remembered my parents daily,
with hearty thanks for their kindness in bringing me
hither. Now, I see it all in a different light. This
gloomy house, which I regarded as the abode of true
life, is a grave, in which I am buried alive. The monk
of Wittenberg has opened my eyes, and I see that all
my pious exercises are but an idle, fruitless endeavor.
Luther's words have startled me out of my dreams.
But he is right, it was but a dream, an imaginary
sanctity. My heart bears me witness to the truth of
his teaching; for God's peace, which I hoped to win
through my devotions and good works,—that I have
never found. I was taught that only in the convent,
true piety had its abiding place. I have learned this
to be false, and I am certain that those who live in
the world can serve God and be saved, as well as we.
Yes, if we who enter here, could leave behind us our
sinful heart ! But that goes with us, and prepares us
trials, of which the world does not dream. It would
seem as though here everything were calculated to
lift the soul above earthly things, and to fill it with

the strength of heavenly life, but in reality, the dreary monotony merely deadens the spirit. Beyond these walls, life shines in bright and happy colors, but here all is gray. There, men rejoice in the lovely Spring-time; they watch for the Summer, which causes the budding germs to flower; they greet the Autumn, with its ripening fruits; and again, when Winter comes, the weary body hails the rest it brings. Here, we scarcely know when the violets are blooming, or when the grapes are gathered, or when the snow is falling. All seasons, all days are alike in this dull life, if indeed it can be called a life. There, men go forth each morning to their day's work, and it is a pleasure to them, a blessing both to body and soul. Their food gives them strength, and their sleep re-freshes them. But our souls and bodies are weakened by this pious idleness. If our convent were in a city, where we could nurse the sick, clothe the naked, com-fort the sorrowing, that would fill the void in our life, and vary its monotony. Ah, Sister Elizabeth, I fear I cannot longer endure the conflict. My strength is failing me, and I feel the blood coursing more and more languidly through my veins.''

She hid her face in her hands. A deep silence suc-ceeded, which Elizabeth did not venture to break. Her tender heart was filled with pity at the sight of

Katharine's misery. She had listened with deep interest, her glowing eyes fixed upon her friend's lips. Strange feelings were awakend within her. Now she rose in great agitation, and grasped Katharine's hand.

"Sister, has God bidden you speak thus to me? Your words have torn the veil from my eyes, and roused thoughts which hitherto slumbered in my soul. You think me happy, Katharine, and you are right, for God has given me a cheerful heart. But yet I am not the trusting child, that accepts with unquestioning confidence the ordinances of the Church, and the rules of our order. Do you suppose that Luther's words have failed to touch me? Since I read his book on 'Monastic Vows' and on the 'Babylonian Captivity,' a thorn has entered my conscience, which torments and terrifies me. My mind is not clear, like yours, to discern the needs of my soul; my trouble has been undefined. But you have put it into words. Now I know what I want, and I am indeed unhappy."

She threw herself upon Katharine's neck and wept aloud. Katharine loosened the clinging arms, and wringing her hands in distress, she exclaimed: "Woe is me! What have I done! Oh, that I had kept silence, and borne my sorrow alone!"

Elizabeth dried her tears, and said, with a gentle caress: "Do not grieve, dear Katharine. It is indeed painful to have one's eyes opened by force. But is it not better to know the truth, than to continue in error?"

After a long and scrutinizing look into her friend's face, Katharine suddenly leaned forward, so that her lips touched Elizabeth's ear. "Elizabeth, you do not know all my trouble."

The young nun's eyes anxiously questioned hers. She continued: "You will not betray me. Elizabeth? I have a secret,—I and seven others."

"Trust me," said Elizabeth.

Katharine drew still nearer and whispered: "Do you know what has happened at Grimma?"

Elizabeth nodded. "How should I not know? The Gospel has been preached there openly, since Luther proclaimed the truth from the pulpit of the town church."

"It is not that I mean," Katharine shook her head. "We have received tidings, that in the past week the monastery of the Holy Cross was deserted by its monks."

Elizabeth started. "What do you say? It is not possible!"

Katharine continued quietly: "These are wonderful times. All signs point to the beginning of a new life. Not at Grimma only, but elsewhere also, the

2

cloisters have opened their gates, after Luther had uttered his Hephatha. Sister Elizabeth,—if our gates were opened,—would you go, or stay?"

A deep crimson dyed Elizabeth's face, and a shiver ran through her body. "Sister, I believe I should go. But," she added drearily, "who will open them? You know how bitterly the abbess hates Luther, and how she rails against him."

A shadow fell upon Katharine's face, and a heavy sigh rose from her breast. "That is my sorrow also. But perhaps the abbess may be forced to yield, whether she will or not."

"I do not understand you," said Elizabeth, in alarm.

Again Katharine leaned over and whispered:— "Eight of the Sisters have entered upon a secret compact. They have written letters to their parents and kinsfolk, imploring them, for God's sake, to pity their condition, and release them from their imprisonment. They say that since they have learned, monastic vows to be opposed to the teachings of Holy Scripture, they should imperil their souls, by continuing to strive after an imaginary sanctity."

Elizabeth's eyes were opened wide. She clutched Katharine's arm and asked eagerly: "Who are they, —these eight?"

Katharine answered: "They are Magdalene von Staupitz, Veronica and Margaret von Zeschau, Laneta von Gohlis, Eva von Gross, Eva and Margaret von Schoenfeld,—I am the eighth."

"Let me be the ninth," pleaded Elizabeth. "If you go, I cannot stay."

For a moment Katharine's eyes scanned the young nun's face, then she said earnestly: "Dear Elizabeth, we will gladly let you share our secret; but be careful, lest you arouse suspicion. Your tongue is quick, and your eyes tell tales."

A sudden flush overspread Elizabeth's face. "Do not fear, dear Katharine. You shall learn that I can keep silence."

Far into the night the nuns sat plying their needles and talking over their plans, until at midnight the little bell again called them to their devotions.

CHAPTER II.

AGAIN it was evening, some weeks later, when seven nuns sat together in the cell of Magdalene von Staupitz. They were very sad, for the hopes, which they had built on the kindness and mercy of their parents and kinspeople, had been miserably disappointed. Magdalene von Staupitz had indeed received from her brother, the Vicar-General of the Augustinian order, a warm and sympathizing letter; and Katharine had just read aloud another from her brother Hans, full of tender, brotherly love; but both urged their sisters not to leave the convent. Monks, they argued, might safely take such a step, being able to work with their hands for their bread. But how would they, poor, helpless nuns, fare in the world? Their second state would be worse than their first.

The other nuns were even more cast down. Their parents had replied with threats and reproaches, and they were so utterly crushed, that it was difficult to console them. Presently, Laneta von Gohlis joined their number, with drooping head and sorrowful eyes.

(20)

Silently she sat down, and the eyes of all sought the face of Magdalene von Staupitz, who was older than the rest, and whose opinion was accepted with the utmost confidence. She had bidden the sisters to her cell, to take counsel with them as to their further course.

Magdalene rose. She was a tall, dignified woman, with a thoughtful face, and a calm manner.

"Our first hope has been put to naught, dear Sisters," she began, in her rich full voice, "and it is a bitter lot, to be forsaken by those whom nature has appointed to be our helpers. They bid us remain. But shall we obey men, rather than God, whose call has come to us through the word of His prophet? Our awakened conscience will not suffer us to continue in a place to which our heart has become a stranger; for all our obedience to the rules and exercises of the order is but hypocrisy."

Katharine von Bora replied, with quivering lips: "My spirit grieves at the thought of ending my days in this dreary place—dead, while yet I am living. But what can we do?"

"Listen to me, sisters—I will tell you my plan," she continued, "since it was Luther, who brought God's Word to us, he is the man to whom we must direct our cry for help—that he may lay it before the throne of God."

"Magdalene," cried Katharine, "how dare we? Should such as we burden the great man with our troubles? Has he not far greater and weightier cares resting upon him?"

Magdalene shook her head. "Do not oppose me, Katharine. Through my brother I have gained more accurate knowledge of the Monk of Wittenberg; and from what I have heard, we will not do amiss in turning to him. His giant spirit does not ask whether persons are of high or low degree; his ears and his heart are open to the needs of the least. Many of the monks, who left their monasteries, have been taken under his protection, and his energetic intercession has secured them a livelihood. Should he not take pity on us, defenceless nuns?"

Eva von Schoenfeld eagerly grasped Magdalene's hand.

"Sister, your advice is good, and new hope has entered my heart. I am sure that Luther will help us. I have absolute faith in him."

A breath of excitement seemed to stir these troubled women. Luther's name revived and strengthened their failing courage, and they crowded around Sister Magdalene, thanking her for her happy, saving thought.

"But how shall Luther hear from us?" asked Eva von Schoenfeld, when the sudden enthusiasm had given place to calm reflection.

"That is the least of our difficulties," replied Magdalene. "Klaus, the gardener, will do the errand for me with pleasure. He has long been waiting for an opportunity to show his gratitude for the help I gave him, when the poisonous insect stung his hand."

Then the door was hastily flung open, and pale as death, Elizabeth von Kanitz rushed into the room.

"All is lost!" she cried, wringing her hands. "My father has come, and in the presence of the abbess, with many reproaches, gave me his answer to my letter. Our secret is betrayed, and I, unhappy girl, have been the cause!"

Burying her face in her hands, she sank upon a stool. The others, speechless, and paralyzed with terror, surrounded her.

Magdaline von Staupitz was the first to recover herself.

"Sisters," she pleaded, "do not lose heart! They will make haste to separate and punish us! We will therefore use the few moments that are left us, and promise each other to abide by our purpose. Now, more than ever, Luther is our only hope. Leave it to me—I will send a messenger to him!"

The nuns had scarcely expressed their assent, when a shuffling step was heard approaching, and presently the abbess stood before the trembling Sisters.

The old woman's face, ordinarily of an ashen hue, had assumed a greenish tint, which was an indication of the deepest anger.   Quivering with rage, she struggled to overcome her agitation sufficiently, to give utterance to her feelings.   For some moments her lips were unable to frame the words, and in anxious silence the nuns, with hands crossed, and heads bowed, stood like criminals, awaiting their doom.   Finally, broken sentences fell from the sanctified lips :

"Oh, that my old eyes should witness such shame ! What have you done, you children of Satan?   If you stood before me—as fallen Magdalens—as murderesses —from my heart I could pity you.   But my soul revolts at your crime, and the sharpest scourge is too gentle for such as you.   Only the day before yesterday, in proud joy, I reported to the General of the order—the convent of Marienthron is an undefiled sanctuary, and proof against heresy.   Now—I am made a liar, my pride is humbled. my glory put to shame !   Holy Mother of God, hide thy face from this iniquity, nor, because of the sin of these nine, do thou punish the whole of this consecrated house.   Their crime shall be visited with heavy punishment, that the stain may be wiped away !   But you—you—you—why do you stand?   On your knees with you !   Into the dust !"

The nuns fell upon their knees, and silently kissed the withered hand of the abbess, in gratitude for the promised punishment—for the convent discipline had taught them to receive punishment as a benefaction.

At· the evening meal, and on the day following, there were nine vacant places in the refectory. The penitents were locked in their cells, on bread and water ; and in the fervor of her holy zeal, the abbess undertook the task of listening at the doors, to make sure that the prisoners recited the prescribed number of prayers. On the fourth day the unhappy nuns were released, but only to be subjected to the deepest humiliation. During the celebration of the Mass, they sat apart from the others, upon the penitent's bench, and while the priest intoned the penitential litany, they were obliged to creep upon their knees to the steps of the altar, striking their breasts with their hands, until the cleansing virtue of holy water and the fumes of incense had dispelled the odor of heresy. The abbess, after they had kissed her feet, then pronounced the formula of absolution, by which they were again received into the fellowship of the children of God. But it was her lips only, that spoke the words—her eyes expressed unappeased hatred, which imparted itself to the other nuns, and made the convent more than ever a hell on earth to the unfortunate heretics.

They were passed by without a glance or a word, and treated as though they had forfeited the right of dwelling in this sacred spot.   They were outlawed, and the bitter need of their hearts, teaching them the insufficiency of prayers learned by rote, constrained them to cast themselves personally before the throne of grace, and like Jacob of old, to wrestle with the Lord in fervent prayer.

.   .   .   .

"Where is Klaus?" asked the abbess of the lay brother, who was busy with his spade among the vegetable beds of the convent garden.

Slowly lifting his head, the brother answered: "He went away to buy seeds."

"Where?"

"He did not tell me—probably to Erfurt."

CHAPTER III.

In a corner house on the market place of Torgau, the merchant Leonhard Koppe, sat at the window of his comfortable room. He was a man past fifty, with a shrewd, kindly face. His head rested on his hand, and his eyes wandered vaguely in the distance. From time to time he moved uneasily in his chair, and passed his hand across his forehead. He seemed to be pondering some weighty matter. His wife, Susanna, had questioned him repeatedly as to his ill humor; but either he answered her curtly, or not at all; until she went away, highly displeased.

Suddenly the merchant rapped at the window, and beckoned eagerly to some one below. A few moments later, a thin, elderly man entered the room. It was the chandler, Master Wolfgang Tommitzsch, whom Leonhard cordially welcomed.

"It was a lucky moment for me, my good neighbor, when you passed my house. You are a man of wise counsel, of which I am sorely in need; therefore I beckoned you to come up to me."

"Say on," replied Master Wolfgang, without moving a muscle of his face. (27)

Leonhard loosened his doublet, and prepared to tell
his trouble. "Yesterday I returned from Wittenberg,
whither I had gone on a matter of business. I also
heard our dear Dr. Luther preach in the church of
St. Mary's—his words still ring in my ears. Afterwards I met Luther, as he was returning from the
church. He suddenly caught me by the sleeve, and
said: 'Ah, is it you, my dear Koppe? My thoughts
were with you this very moment—and here I see you
actually before me, as though you had dropped from
heaven. This, it seems to me, is of God's ordering,
and is a sign to me, that you are the man to carry out
the business which weighs upon my mind. You are
acquainted in the convent of Nimptschen?' When I
told him that I supplied the order with cloth and wax,
he continued: 'Listen to me. In the convent are
nine noble maidens who are weary of their nunnery,
but do not know how to obtain their liberty. In their
need, after they had in vain petitioned their kinsfolk,
they turned to me for help—which I would gladly
give, but that my arm is too short to reach from Wittenberg to Nimptschen. Neither could I go thither
myself and liberate the poor captives, either secretly
or by force. Therefore I have need of a man who
will lend me his arm, and I ask you, Master Koppe,
to do it, for the love of God. You know the road,

and have a clear head to devise ways and means, and a good Christian heart that can pity the misery of others. Will you undertake this matter?' And I said yes,—for who can resist the magic of Luther's wonderful lightning eyes, and the pleading of his voice? I was proud indeed that he stood and talked with me thus publicly—the great man, who fears neither pope nor devil.

"But when he had gone, I felt hot and cold, for I perceived that I had built a tower without reckoning the cost. I pondered the matter on my homeward journey, and here I still sit and torment myself. The closer I look at it, the more ticklish it appears. How shall I disclose my plan to the nuns, without arousing the suspicions of the abbess? Notwithstanding her seventy years, she has the eyes of a lynx, and the scent of a fox. Even if I should succeed in approaching them unperceived, how will it be possible to get them away? If it were one, or even two, it might be done—but a whole wagon full! And when they are safely out of the convent, we must still pass through the territory of Duke George ; and that is a dangerous journey, inasmuch as the Duke hates Luther more than he hates the Devil himself. Dear friend, what say you?"

Tommitzsch half closed his eyes and nodded re-

flectively. After a moment's thought, he looked up
and said: "The distress of these nuns touches my
heart. Only lately I witnessed the joy of my sister's
child, who escaped from the convent at Wurzen. Such
may be the joy of a person who rises from his grave;
and methinks it is a good work, and well pleasing to
God, to help a human being from death to life. I
pity the nuns at Nimptschen, although they are strangers to me; and if Dr. Martin desires it, how can we
hesitate? Therefore, neighbor, make the venture,
and I will give you my help."

"For which you have my hearty thanks," cried the
merchant, wringing his friend's hand. "If you devise the plan, it will surely succeed."

The chandler answered calmly: "It is a good work
—and God will aid us. When do you carry the next
load of goods to the convent?"

"The order may come at any hour, for Easter is
near at hand," replied Master Leonhard. "What do
you mean?"

Tommitzsch returned: "It must be an easy matter
to deliver a letter secretly to one of the nuns."

The merchant listened attentively, and after a little
more conversation, the chandler left the house.

On the following morning, a heavy, canvas-covered
wagon rumbled along the road from Torgau to Grim-

ma, and, on the evening of the same day, halted at
the gates of the convent Marienthron at Nimptschen,
about the time when the nuns were walking in the garden, after their evening meal.

Such an arrival from the busy world was an important event amid the monotony of convent life, especially when it was Master Leonhard Koppe from Torgau—the pleasant, talkative man, who brought an
abundance of news, and related such merry tales.
For strange to say, these brides of heaven greatly rel-
ished an earthly jest.

As usual, he was soon surrounded by the nuns, and
amid much cheerful talk unpacked his wares. But his
eyes seemed to be seeking some one; he was absent-
minded, and failed to answer their questions. When
at last Magdalene von Staupitz, coming in from the
garden, approached the group, he grew taciturn, and
gave them to understand he was not in the mood for
conversation.

As Magdalene came nearer, a quick glance from
the merchant's eyes met hers. She turned away, to
hide the flush which rose to her face; and, returning
to the garden, concealed herself behind an alder-
bush near the entrance, from whence she could overlook the court.

After the nuns had dispersed, she again drew near,

and sought to find in the merchant's face an explanation of his look. Hidden from the convent by his
great wagon, he hastily gave her a letter, saying:
"Read it. At the appointed time I shall be at hand."

He then climbed into the wagon, to prepare himself
a resting place for the night, and the nun disappeared
among the shadows. ·

·   ·   ·   ·   ·   ·   ·   ·   ·   ·

"What ails you, Sister Magdalene?" questioned the
abbess, later in the evening. "Are you ill? Your
face is pale, and the rosary trembles in your hands."

Magdalene cast down her eyes, and answered softly:
"I feel as though a fever were shaking me. My prayers wearied me, and my head is dull and confused."

"Then see to it that some tea is made for you,"
said the abbess.

Obediently, the nun left the presence of the dreaded superior, hastily swallowed the nauseous drink, and
sought her cell to escape the torture of further questioning. She found Katharine von Bora awaiting her.

"Tell me, sister," exclaimed Katharine, "what has
happened? My heart beats with fear, but I dared not
ask you in the presence of the others."

With a sigh of relief, Magdalene bolted her door,
then sank trembling into Katharine's arms. "Katha-

rine, dear Katharine, the day dawns,—the day of freedom! Luther—Luther—O thou prophet of the Most
High, thou deliverer of the German people, thou wilt
prove our good angel also!"

Katharine shivered within Magdalene's encircling
arms.

"Do not speak in riddles, sister," she cried. "Relieve me from this suspense."

Magdalene drew a slip of paper from her bosom.
"See here; the answer to our petition to Dr. Martin.
Leonhard Koppe, the merchant, gave it to me secretly. It is difficult to decipher, for Master Koppe's
hand is not skilled in writing. Listen to what he
says : 'Dr. Martin greets the nine Sisters, and through
me, Leonhard Koppe, the merchant of Torgau, will
restore them to liberty. Therefore, hold yourselves
in readiness. In the night before Easter, on the
fourth of April, at the hour of ten, I will be under
Katharine von Bora's window, from whence escape is
easiest. Do what is needful to keep the secret, and
may the Almighty have mercy on you!'"

Katharine would have cried out for joy, but Magdalene's hand sealed her lips. "Restrain yourself, sister. If God is preparing a path of escape for us, our
own imprudence must not throw obstacles in the way.
Consider,—our salvation or ruin lies in our own hands.

3

Woe be to us, if we betray ourselves and our deliverers.''

"What did you say?" interrupted Katharine, excitedly. "In the night before Easter? God pity us! Is not that, of all times, the most unsuitable?"

"You mean because of the vigil?" asked Magdalene, reflecting. Then after another glance at the letter, her eyes beamed afresh. "No,—that very night will be the most favorable to our plans. The vigil begins at midnight, and on that evening we retire earlier than usual to get a few hours of sleep. Here I read, that the merchant from Torgau will wait for us at the hour of ten. Is not that wisely planned? Oh, my spirit rises with new courage, kindled by hope, and my last doubts are silenced.''

Overcome by her feelings, Magdalene fell upon her knees, and from the depths of her heart came her thanksgiving: "Thou Lord of my life, Thou God of my salvation, I thank Thee, that Thou hast guided a heart to accomplish our deliverance. I put my trust in Thee, Who wilt surely finish the work Thou hast begun, for Thy Name's sake. Amen.''

CHAPTER IV.

FREEDOM.

IT was Easter Eve in the year 1523. After the solemn hush of Good Friday, a bustling activity stirred the little community. The work was done in silence, it is true, for the day on which the body of our Lord lay in the sepulchre, demanded quiet and reverence; but all hands were busy with preparations worthy of the highest festival of the Christian Church. Groups of nuns were binding wreaths of moss and cedar-branches, with which to deck the images of the Saints and the life-size statue of the blessed Virgin, which occupied the most prominent place in the chapel. Others were engaged about the altar, which on Good Friday had been stripped of all ornament. They covered it with a cloth of white silk embroidered in gold, and supplied the candlesticks with fresh tapers, which Leonhard Koppe had lately provided. Others were building up in the altar recess a representation of the Resurrection,—the grave, surrounded by the prostrate watchers, and the Saviour issuing from its portal, bearing aloft the banner of victory.

(35)

The forenoon passed amid these preparations.

The mid-day meal was eaten in silence, for the strict fast permitted but scanty refreshment. During the afternoon the convent was silent as the grave. The nuns, weary in body and mind from the exertions of Holy Week, rested in their cells. Since Palm Sunday, they had spent but few hours in their beds, having been engaged day and night in praying, fasting, singing, confessing and hearing mass. Many may therefore have rejoiced in the blessed Easter day,—not only because our Lord was risen from the dead for the saving of the world, but also because the tired and enfeebled body might once more assert its rights, and the soul awaken from its spiritual weariness to a new life.

Slowly the twilight fell upon the earth. Once more the bell called to prayers, and the stewardess summoned the nuns to the thin, gray, Lenten soup. Then the last sound died away in the convent. The tired devotees stretched their aching limbs upon their beds, to find in slumber a little strength for the last effort, —the Easter vigil,—that night service, which with mysterious premonition leads the soul upward, step by step, to the supreme moment, when the first ray of the rising sun startles the soft murmurs into jubilant praise, and from the full choir, accompanied by trumpets and cymbals, the Easter hymn bursts forth:

" Christ the Lord is risen
From His martyr prison,
Let us all rejoice in this,
Christ our joy and solace is.
Kyrie eleison."

.   .   .   .

The night was damp and cold. A bitter wind drove
the ragged clouds across the face of the moon, whose
pale beams threw ghostly shadows upon the earth. In
the forest the trees groaned and creaked, their branches tossed by the gale.

A great wagon, loaded with barrels, moved slowly
along the road leading from Torgau. When the
clouds did not hide the moon, three muffled figures,
sitting immovable upon the wagon, became visible.

Near the convent they left the highway. One of
the men sprang down and took the horses by the
bridle.

" Do you know the road, neighbor?" came a whisper from within.

" Have no fear," was the answer. " I know every
path. Follow me, until we reach the water. There
we will leave the wagon among the alders. You,
Caspar, stay with the horses and care for them."

Caspar was Leonhard's nephew. When they reached

the pond they stopped. Caspar fed and watered the
horses, while the others carefully groped their way
through the bushes, Koppe taking his friend's hand,
to help him because of his uncertain eyesight, and
because the pale rays of the moon, which flickered
through the trees, threw but scant light upon their
path.

"Do you see yonder garden wall?" whispered
Koppe. "I will creep on it to the spot, where it
meets the building. There, where the light is shining,
is Katharine von Bora's cell. I am glad to see that
all the other windows are dark. My supposition was
correct,—the nuns are sleeping until midnight. But
it is not yet ten o'clock. Let us see if all is safe.
The abbess is still awake," he grumbled, when they
had reached the eastern front of the convent. "The
venerable ghost has no peace, and often startles the
nuns by her sudden appearances. She is a strange
woman, and in her dealings with me, has given me
much trouble by her suspicion and avarice. In her
own eyes she is a saint, whose good works are so many
that they reach up into Heaven, like the tower of
Babel. Therefore she has much confidence and courage, and fears nothing, save the screech-owl, whose cry
so grates upon her nerves, that in the Springtime she
pays a golden florin for every owl's egg that is brought
her."

Tommitzsch murmured something that sounded like a succession of maledictions. Suddenly he stopped, and seized his friend by the arm.

" I am not going any further with you."

" Why not ?" asked Koppe, in dismay.

Tommitzsch replied in his imperturbable manner : " You can forego my help in your kidnapping business. I can imitate the cry of the screech-owl," he explained, " as well as that of the hawk and the cat. When the time has come, I will be the bird that turns her bravery into fear. In the meantime, you do your work."

".Truly, you are a wise counsellor," said Koppe, tapping his friend on the shoulder. " I am glad that I sought your assistance. It wants but a few minutes to ten."

The men grasped each other by the hand, each with hearty good wishes for the success of the other.

With redoubled caution, Koppe stole along the wall, until he reached a spot where a few crumbling stones gave him a foothold. Here he climbed up, and softly crept along the top. Suddenly, a sharp cry, piercing the silence, reached his ear. He started in alarm, but soon smiled at his fears.

" The screech-owl," he said to himself. The cry was repeated at intervals, and in the meantime, Koppe

had reached the lighted window.   He rose to his feet,
—but alas! it was beyond the reach of his outstretched
hand.   He had been deceived in the height.   How
was he to make himself heard?   Calling was out of
the question.   And how would they descend?   He
struck with his fist upon the wall, but the sound of
his blows died away against the solid masonry.   Then
he bethought him of a key which he carried in his
pocket.   With this he tapped, and it rang clear against
the stones.

Hark!   They are moving overhead.   The window
is softly opened and a head is thrust out.

"Your rescuer is here!" he whispered, and the answer came back, "God be praised!"

The head was withdrawn, soon to re-appear, and
Koppe heard the words: "Wait, until we fasten the
rope to the casement."

The complaint he was about to utter, died upon his
lips.   Woman's wit had planned with better fore-
thought, than manly wisdom.   In less than a minute
the end of the rope struck his head,—another minute,
and the first nun stood beside him.

"Creep carefully forward," he directed the trembling girl, "I will receive the others."

Again the screech-owl shrieked.   No other sound
was heard, save the creaking of the branches in the

wind. In wild haste the nuns slipped down, and crept along the wall. Koppe followed. When they came to the breach, he sprang down and assisted them to ascend. A suppressed cry of delight was heard, but Koppe angrily checked the guilty one.

"The time for rejoicing has not yet come! Make haste, and follow!"

The wagon was soon reached, and the merchant hid the nuns between the barrels, covering them with straw, until not a sign of them was visible. Then he hastened to relieve his companion from his post. They climbed into the wagon, and the horses were urged forward.

Dark and shadowy, like a gigantic sarcophagus, the convent lay behind them. Not a light gleamed from the windows, even that of the abbess being dark. The effect of the screech-owl's voice had not been miscalculated, and the old woman had doubtless sought refuge beneath her covers from the gruesome cries of the bird of death.

The nuns crouched motionless in their hiding place —afraid to utter a sound. Like a mill-stone the reaction from the past dangers, and the fear of new ones weighed upon their spirits. Thus they journeyed for more than an hour. Suddenly the wagon stopped, and a harsh voice called to the driver: "What have you here?"

"Herring barrels," was Koppe's short and decided answer. "Do not detain me unnecessarily, friend— my limbs are stiff with the cold."

The man climbed up at the side of the wagon, and gropingly examined its contents.

"Pass on!" he cried, and the horses hurried forward at a more rapid pace.

Suddenly there was a stirring and a whispering among the straw, Koppe and Tommitzsch now and then adding a word of caution. The nuns would fain have risen from their stifling shelter, and thanked the men who had dared so much for their deliverance, but they forbade it. After a few hours, when the sky grew rosy in the east, and the first fiery ray of the Easter sun broke upon the earth, new life stirred the nuns with irresistible force, and as with one voice, the exultant strain burst forth from their lips :

> "Christ the Lord is risen
> From His martyr prison,
> Let us all rejoice in this,
> Christ our joy and solace is,
> Kyrie eleison."

Leonhard had lifted his hand with a warning gesture, but it sank at his side. His eyes filled with tears as he listened ; the pure voices had a heavenly ring. Nor did he resist, when the nuns pressed around him, took his hands, and overwhelmed him and his companions with their gratitude.

In the holy fervor of her enthusiasm, Katharine von Bora stretched forth her hands and cried: "Easter! Easter! Thou name full of joy and of life! Hear our resurrection hymn, thou Saviour, who hast had mercy on us. We were dead, and behold, we live! The grave has yielded up its prey, and with the golden Easter sun, life sends us its greeting! Hallelujah! O thou world, from which I fled, receive me once more; for vanity and delusion is the sanctity of convent life. Receive me, O world, shone upon by God's sun, and peopled with living beings! In thee, more worthily than in the nun's habit will I serve my God! Lord of the world, Thy kingdom is wide, Thou wilt doubtless have in it a place for poor Katharine!"

CHAPTER V.

THE month of May had come. In the Burgomaster's street, in Wittenberg, stood a high-gabled house, ornamented with two fierce dragon heads. There the syndic, Master Philip Reichenbach, and his wife were seated near a window enjoying the twilight—the sweetest hour of the twenty-four to the master of the house —when, after the labors of the day, he could enjoy the peaceful quiet of his home.

Master Reichenbach was a short, thick-set man, near fifty, and highly esteemed in Wittenberg for his calm judgment and honorable mind. His wife Elsa, a refined, energetic little woman, had doubtless been a great beauty in her youth; and even now it was a pleasure to look into her fresh, kindly face, to whose delicate features the inner beauty of the soul had given their final charm.

The arrangement of the house bore evidence of great wealth; but the spacious halls were silent; no merry, childish voices disturbed the stillness. So much the more were husband and wife drawn to each other. (44)

"At last the Doctor has found a shelter for the remaining two of the escaped nuns," the syndic reported.

"The Zeschau sisters?" asked Frau Elsa, with lively interest. "I thank God, for the dear Doctor's sake. I have pitied him from my heart. It is a mystery to me, how he will carry through all the business that rests upon him. Another had broken down long ago under the burden. His convent is like a dovecote, where there is a continual coming and going. Who can count the letters he writes? And must he not, as from a high watch-tower, overlook all things, like a king of the spiritual world, taking note of the smallest, as well as of the weightiest matters? I am vexed with the people who trouble him with their small affairs, and waste his precious time. I was angry with the nuns at Nimptschen, when I heard that they had petitioned Dr. Martin; and when, not content with having been released from their prison, they came hither to trouble him further. I am comforted, now that his unceasing efforts have procured a shelter for them all—not only comforted, but glad and thankful, inasmuch as by these means, our dear Kate has become a member of our household."

The syndic, well pleased with this turn of his wife's speech, contentedly rubbed his knees and said: "I

am glad of it, dear Elsa. I was fearful, lest the
guest, whom we received for Luther's sake, might
prove burdensome to you, and disturb the quiet of
our household. I feared also that you might be ill-
suited to one another, for Katharine von Bora is of a
different temper from you."

A happy smile played around Frau Elsa's lips.
"All my care has been turned into pleasure. You
are right,—Katharine's temper and inner disposition
are different from mine. There is something so noble
and great-hearted in her character, that I often feel
myself small in comparison. At times she seems
proud and haughty, as even Dr. Luther lately re-
marked. But her pride is only maidenly dignity,—
the expression of her high and noble mind. And
withal, her eyes meet the world with a glance so clear
and ¡open, her words are so straightforward, and her
judgment so true, that often I am fain to ask her counsel. She is like a child, in her innocent happiness;
and often she falls upon my neck, kisses me, and ex-
claims: 'Ah, how happy I am; and I owe it all to
you and to the great Doctor.' She always calls Luther the 'great Doctor,' and when we speak of him,
she listens reverently with folded hands. As in former days she reverenced the saints of the Romish
calendar, so she now venerates Dr. Martin, holding

him to be greater and more glorious than many of those whom the Church has canonized.

"You should see her, dear Philip, when she is busied with household duties. I feared at first, that she would cause me much unwonted labor; but now, my hands often lie idle, because I find my work already done. She reads my wishes in my eyes, and her hand is skillful and quick in learning the unaccustomed duties. I often think, as I watch her: Happy is the man, whom this Martha will serve! and a feeling of envy creeps into my heart, for I would rather keep her with me always, and I dread the day when the wooers will appear."

"Are you thinking of Jerome Baumgaertner, the young patrician from Nuremberg?" asked her husband. "Methinks you are needlessly troubled. I saw indeed how his eyes followed Katharine, when on your Name day he sat at table with us, and I notice that since then his visits are unnecessarily frequent. But Katharine is timid in her intercourse with men. You know that, although she has been four weeks in our house, she can scarcely be persuaded to leave it, except to go to church."

Elsa shook her head, regarding her husband with a compassionate smile: "I understand a woman's heart better than you. Modesty and reserve are a maiden's

loveliest adornments, and in a man's eyes they are an
added charm, urging him to pluck the flowers that
seem beyond his reach. The young man seems not
to displease Katharine; and she dreads to leave the
shelter of our house, not because of those who love
her, but because of her enemies and detractors. She
has heard the evil things that were said about the nuns
of Nimptschen, although I tried to conceal them from
her. She knows also that the merchant Leonhard
Koppe, of Torgau, is in great danger from the anger
of the Papists, and that Dr. Luther addressed to him
a public letter of thanks for his brave deed. This is
her reason for shunning intercourse with strangers.
But it will not always be thus."

The rosy glow of the sunset shone through the
round panes, and the pictures on the wall, painted by
the hand of Master Lucas Kranach, were tinged with
a golden light.

"How clear the sunset, and how fair the evening!"
said the syndic. "Let us walk in the garden until
supper is served. Have the peas been planted? It
should have been done yesterday, but I found no
time."

Frau Elsa did not know. They crossed the spacious hall and courtyard, and entered the garden,
which covered a large piece of ground. To the right

was planted an orchard of fruit-trees, and to the left were borders already prepared for vegetables and flowers.

A kneeling figure was busily engaged before one of the freshly dug beds.

"Is this Katharine?" exclaimed Reichenbach in surprise, as the figure hastily arose. "My dear Katharine, what are you doing here?" he asked.

With a smile, the girl replied: "The peas looked at me so questioningly, whether I would not prepare for them their little bed in the earth; and the leaves of the cabbage plants hung limp, so that it was high time to plant them."

The syndic's eyes rested for a moment upon her work. "But who has taught you this? And those slender fingers, that from childhood have been clasped in prayer, or telling beads, are they fit for such coarse work?"

Katharine glanced at him and said: "Love is a good teacher. One learns quickly, what one does willingly."

"But you should spare yourself, lest you overtax your strength," warned the syndic.

Katharine shook her head. "Did you spare yourself, when you permitted the strange, runaway nun, to disturb the quiet of your household? Ah, I wish I

4

could do much more to requite your Christian charity!
It is my daily prayer, that God may pay poor Katharine's debt.''

An expression of deep gratitude animated her
face, and made it almost beautiful. Frau Elsa silently
clasped the girl in her arms, while her husband turned
into another path to hide his emotion.

As he walked through the garden, he saw on all
sides traces of a busy hand, that had cleared the paths,
plucked up the weeds and tended the flowers. He did
not need to ask, whose hand it was; and with hearty
pleasure his eyes followed Katharine, who, her arm
linked in that of his wife, was walking before him.

Soon Sybilla, the old servant, came to announce
Dr. Luther, who presently appeared, clad in his dark-
colored, monkish gown.

"God's greeting to you, my dear friend," he exclaimed. "How goes it with you? And how fares
our poor little nun?"

The syndic reverently lifted his hat, and offered his
hand in welcome to his guest. "Have no fear for
her, Doctor, it goes well with her."

"But you, my friend,—will she not be burdensome
to you? You are making a great sacrifice for my
sake; and I am troubled when I think that you may
be further inconvenienced. I wish some one would

come and make a wife of the maiden,—that is more
truly a woman's vocation.''

With a serious face, the syndic answered: ''Most
reverend Doctor, you have done so much for us. Will
you do one thing more? Do not allow this to trouble
you. It is no sacrifice, to keep Katharine; but it
would grieve us to part with her, for she has become
dear to us as our own child.''

Luther's worn face was lighted with a ray of pleasure. Clasping his friend's hand, he said: ''A true
friend is a precious treasure, and not to be bought
with gold. Continue to be my friend always. As for
me, I shall hold you dearer than ever, from this day
forth.'' Meanwhile the women had approached.
Katharine, when she saw the monk, sought timidly to
draw Frau Elsa away, whispering: ''The great Doctor!'' But the little lady was not to be restrained
from welcoming the beloved guest.

Luther's eyes rested with pleased surprise upon the
graceful figure of the former nun, in whose pale cheeks
the air of freedom had caused the first spring-roses to
bloom. With a smile he noted the traces of her work
still clinging to her dress.

''Ah, Mistress Katharine,'' he jested, ''you have
indeed become a child of the world. And how does
it please you? I see that your mind turns to earthly

things, and that you busy yourself with mean and
lowly matters, which draw your thoughts to the dust,
for soiled are both your dress and hand.   Would you
not rather return to the convent, where you would be
far removed from an evil world, while your thoughts
floated heavenward upon clouds of incense?"

Katharine's cheeks grew rosier still, as she answered
softly, with downcast eyes: "Leave me in the world;
it is beautiful here.   Surely so long as I am not of the
world, I can serve God acceptably, and dedicate my
life to Him.   From your own lips I have learned, that
the dear Lord is served with small things, as well as
with great."

The Doctor was about to answer, when Frau Elsa
forestalled him, with the request that he would remain
to supper.

Luther met her eyes with a merry glance.   "How
skillfully you have divined my thoughts.   Had you
not bidden me stay, I should have offered myself as
your guest, otherwise I had gone supperless to bed;
for my servant, Wolfgang, but an hour ago, came to
my cell with a very long face, saying: 'Doctor, what
will you eat this evening?   There was a remnant of
baked fish in the larder, which would have served for
your supper; but a cat must have eaten it, for nothing is left but a few bones.' "

With deep sympathy, Katharine looked up to the man, who in such rich measure broke the bread of life to all the world, and yet lacked daily bread for his own need. Her admiration rose at the greatness of his mind, which could turn his poverty into a jest. She whispered her thoughts to Frau Elsa, who answered in the same tone: "He has barely enough for the necessities of life. His professor's salary is but twenty-two thalers and twelve groschen, and he forgets his own wants, to give to the many poor, who daily importune his generous heart."

"His life must be dreary enough," Katharine continued, "in his gloomy convent, where no woman's hand can minister to his comfort. Wolfgang may be faithful,—but he is no woman."

They entered the hall, where Sybilla had served the evening meal.

"Would you hear some news, my friends?" said Luther, when they were seated. "Leonhard Koppe, the robber of nuns, for whom the Papists would fain prepare a heretic's death, rather deserves a martyr's crown; for behold, the deed which he ventured in God's name, has been followed by great blessing. It was of no avail, to conceal what had happened at Nimptschen. The tidings penetrated into other convents, and our dear Kate has found many imitators.

To-day I learned, that nine nuns, together with their abbess, escaped from the Benedictine convent at Zeitz, six nuns from the abbey at Sarmitz, eight from the Cistercian convent of Bentlitz, and sixteen from the Dominican house of Widerstedt. Mistress Katharine will doubtless rejoice to hear, that three more nuns left Nimptschen,—not secretly, but were taken away in orderly fashion by their kinspeople. I am heartily glad of it. But in order that the convent gates may be opened more freely still, I am writing the history of Florentina von Oberweimar, who fled from the nunnery of Neuhelfta, near Eisleben. This little book will be printed and spread abroad, that all the world may learn what is a nun's life; that the Devil's wiles may be exposed, and that poor Leonhard Koppe may hereafter be left in peace.''

Frau Elsa passed a dish to the Doctor, and pressed him to eat. ''These are good tiding, reverend sir, and our dear Kate seems well pleased. I will ask you to lend me the history of Florentina, as soon as it is printed. But do not forget that this is the time to eat. You need some nourishment, for the dark shadows under your eyes tell of sleepless nights and over-much study.''

Luther mechanically put some of the food on his plate, and said: ''For that the godless prophets of

Zwickau are to blame, who, while I sat imprisoned as Squire George, laid waste the vineyard of the Lord; and it is more laborious to build up than to destroy. Many a morning, when I look at my untouched bed, I think of Karlstadt, and say: 'Behold, for this friendly service I have to thank thee!'"

"But tell me, Doctor," said Frau Elsa, "how do you accomplish all this work, which would tax the strength of ten men? You preach, lecture, write books, translate the Bible, receive and answer letters, —yet you never grow weary, and always have a cheerful heart. You find time to help Wolfgang at his lathe, to tend the flowers in your garden, and to hold converse with your friends."

Luther looked up with a pleasant smile. "Dear friend, for the accomplishment of such labors two things are needful,—order and prayer. Has not each hour sixty minutes? Much can be done in sixty minutes, if we do it in order, redeeming the time. And prayer is a fresh well, from whence body and soul draw ever new strength. This Psalter"—and he drew a little book from his breast-pocket,—"is my constant companion and comforter, from whom I learn and receive all that I need. I hold my prayers to be stronger by far than all the Devil's might and cunning; and if for one day I forget to pray, my faith would grow cold. Work and pray evermore, and God will help thee !''

Katharine listened with reverent attention. Then she bent her head and whispered : '' The great Doctor ! The wonderful man ! Oh, to have him always before one's eyes, and to follow his example ! If I might but be his servant.'' A warm glance from Frau Elsa, and a soft pressure of the hand was her answer.

Doctor Martin then entered into a conversation with the syndic, regarding the Knight Franz von Sickingen, whose tragic end had saddened many hearts. The strong man had been conquered by a stronger. The princes of Hesse, Palatinate and Treves, had besieged and overpowered his fortress of Landstuhl.

'' I was almost vexed with you, Doctor,'' said the syndic, ''when you refused Sickingen's proffered hand. His good sword, I trusted, would prove a strong defence, and hew a way for the Gospel, despite the Pope and the Emperor ; for Sickengen's power was growing apace. Now it is clear to me, that in this matter also you were in the right.''

Luther shook his head sadly. '' I grieve for thee, my brother Sickingen ! He meant it well with me. And yet he was a tempter, to whom I must needs say :

Get thee behind me, who, with carnal weapons, wouldst further God's sacred cause ! Such means are ill-pleasing to the Lord, and endanger the truth, which needs no earthly props or crutches, having within itself the power to conquer the world. It is the *Word*, which must achieve the victory, not the *Sword !* Had I entrusted the Gospel to Sickingen's hand, it would have perished with the dying hero. But it is time that I go, for Wolfgang and the nun Florentina are awaiting me at home. Will you not give me something for the poor fellow? He is so faithful, and would share his last morsel with me ! "

Before Frau Elsa could rise, Katharine had wrapped a piece of smoked meat in a napkin, and given it to Doctor Martin. He thanked them, and wished them good-night.

CHAPTER VI.

A FLEETING FANCY.

It was in August of the same year, 1523, when Frau Elsa entered her husband's room one morning in great haste. Her cheeks glowed, her breath came fast, and for some moments she was unable to speak.

"I have discovered who it is, that every morning leaves a nosegay at the window. It is as I suspected."

The syndic rubbed his eyes and stared at his wife. "You mean the youth from Nuremberg?"

"No other! He has been very bold of late. In church he places himself near her, and disturbs her devotions with his attentions—it is sinful! And Kate seems not disinclined to favor his suit. Only the other day, when we supped with Lucas Kranach, she had much conversation with young Baumgaertner, who was among the guests. On the way home, she asked me if it were far from here to Nuremberg, and whether all Suabians were as hearty in their speech, as this young Jerome?

"What reply did you make?"

"I told her the road was very long from here to Nuremberg, and that I was not aware that the speech of the Suabians was more hearty than that of the Saxons ; but this I knew—a man's friendly words were no proof that his heart was true. She answered not a word, but gave me an embarrassed, questioning look."

"I trust she understood your meaning. It would grieve me to give her to Jerome. If we must needs part with her, I hope it may be to a worthy man, in whom we have confidence. This young gentleman seems to be of a light and frivolous disposition."

"I think the same," replied Elsa, with a lively gesture. "But I believe that Doctor Luther is fond of the youth. He has repeatedly praised him for his industry, and for the abundant knowledge he has acquired at the University. I fear that Jerome will find a warm advocate in Luther."

"Dearest Elsa," said the syndic, laying his hand on his wife's shoulder, "here our experience must needs come to the aid of youthful ignorance. Katharine is to us as our own child, and we would sin, did we not endeavor to save her from unhappiness and heart-ache. I can easily believe that her heart inclines to the youth—he is of a handsome figure, has good manners, and is moreover the first man who has approached her with professions of love. If she knew more of men, she would be more cautious."

Frau Elsa ended the conversation, and urged her husband to be ready for morning prayers.

As Sybilla was bringing in the morning meal, three loud knocks were heard at the door, and presently a handsome, richly-dressed youth appeared. Bowing with courtly grace, he stood upon the threshold, awaiting the master's permission to enter.

"You honor us at an early hour, Master Baumgaertner," said the syndic, with some embarrassment, rising and offering his hand to the visitor, while Frau Elsa, in confused haste, busied herself about the table.

The young man replied : " Pardon me, if I disturb you, but because of my sudden departure, I found no more suitable time to bid you farewell."

Reichenbach looked up at the tall youth with surprise, and Frau Elsa drew nearer. "What do you say ? You are going to leave Wittenberg ?"

Nodding assent, the student explained: " It is hard for me to leave the place where I have experienced so much pleasure and benefit—yet I owe obedience to my father, who demands my speedy return."

With hypocritical warmth and ill-concealed pleasure Frau Elsa urged the young man to share the repast ; inquired with much feeling as to the reasons of the paternal command, and was altogether so friendly and

affable, that he was surprised to find himself thus suddenly received into favor by one who had always treated him with chilling reserve. His eyes often wandered toward the door, as though he expected some one,
and the longer he waited, the more restless were his
glances, and the more confused his answers.

At last he rose to go. It was evident that something weighed upon his mind, to which his tongue refused to give utterance, until with a heroic effort, he
plucked up courage to ask after Katharine.

"I should like to bid her farewell, if I—"

His sentence was left unfinished ; the embarrassment
which it produced increasing his own diffidence.

After a painful silence, Frau Elsa stammered :—
"Doubtless she has not slept well, or she would have
appeared at morning prayers. If you have any message for her, I will gladly be the bearer of it."

A shadow fell upon the young man's handsome face.
His lips parted, so that the white teeth became visible
under his brown beard, and with anxious questioning
his eyes rested upon the face of the lady, who grew hot
and cold under his glance. Her husband's voice
sounded almost like a reproof when he said :

"Go and see why Katharine delays so long." With
inward reluctance Frau Elsa turned to obey, when the
door was opened and Katharine appeared. At the

sight of the young man, she started and blushed.

The syndic came to her relief. Taking her hand in a fatherly fashion, he said: "Come hither, Katharine, and greet Master Baumgaertner, who has come to take leave of us before he returns to his home."

Katharine's face grew pale, and her. eyes timidly sought those of the young man, who approached, and would have taken her hand.

"I pray you, dear lady, remember me kindly, as I will also faithfully keep you in my memory, until God so orders it, that I may see your face again."

"You will then return to Wittenberg?" both women asked, in one breath—the one with glad surprise, the other in visible dismay.

With a burst of enthusiasm, the young man exclaimed: "How could I forget Wittenberg! Here my mind was nourished, and my heart awakened. Not long, I trust, will dutiful obedience detain me in Nuremburg; then I shall hasten to return hither. In the meantime I commit you to God's keeping."

He paused, to conceal the emotion which overpowered him, and after a very hasty leave-taking, hurried away.

On this and the following day, deep silence reigned in the syndic's house. Husband and wife had little to say to one another, and overhead, in her little chamber, sat Katharine, lonely and sorrowful. Her heart seemed empty. Now that Jerome had gone away, she became aware of the warmth of her feeling for him. She resolved to take comfort in the affection of her friends, but this seemed an insufficient substitute ; and she had a strong foreboding that Jerome would not return. Yet, when the hot tears would have burst from her eyes, she struggled with all her strength against her sorrow, lest the syndic and his wife might perceive that her love was shared by another, whose suit they disapproved. She felt it as a sin, that her benefactors should yield to a stranger, because, forsooth, he had approached her with friendly words and glances. " Be still, foolish heart," she said, " and see to it, if with redoubled love thou canst expiate thy wrong against these kind friends."

Shortly after, Frau Elsa received her husband one evening with a lively welcome : " Philip, our Kate is a brave girl ! She has conquered her own heart, and is once more wholly ours ! "

CHAPTER VII.

KATHARINE IN TROUBLE, AND DR. MARTIN IN STRIFE WITH HIS FRIENDS.

MORE than a year had passed. The Autumn of 1524 had come, busily destroying whatever the summer had wrought. In the streets the wind played his pranks with the first fallen leaves. On the housetops the swallows held noisy counsel together, as to their flight to the sunny Southern land, whither the storks had already preceded them.

It was Sunday morning. Crowds streamed from the town church at Wittenberg, where Luther had preached. In eager groups they stood about the market-place; and noticeable among these was the syndic, Philip Reichenbach, engaged in lively conversation with a courtly looking man in a rich dress, whose handsome, intelligent face was of a rare, artistic type. A long beard fell down upon his breast. This was the court-painter and Senator, Lucas Kranach.

"I scarcely trusted my eyes," exclaimed the syndic, eagerly gesticulating, "when I saw Brother Martin appear in the priest's frock, instead of his monkish

(64)

habit. My heart rejoices, for the ugly cowl no longer suited him. After he has inwardly put away the monk's life, why should he continue to wear its outward sign ? The old gown, worn and threadbare as it is, has earned its rest. But it pleases me little that he continues in the monastery, when all the monks, save the Prior Eberhard Brisger, have gone away. It were better he broke with all monkish habits."

" It is well known, dear friend," said Kranach, " that Dr. Martin has small regard for outward appearances. He may have good reasons for continuing in the convent. It is said that the Elector intends to make him a gift of it."

The syndic opened his eyes. " What ! and would he receive such a gift ? "

" Why not ? " asked the other. " It is an evidence of favor on the Elector's part."

" Hm," said Reichenbach, " as you take it. There he sits, alone in the great, dreary, half-ruined house, with no woman's hand to minister to his wants. All that he teaches concerning the blessed Gospel is clear and plain to me ; as he teaches, so he lives ; and if anything in his words seemed difficult to understand, it is made clear by his life. But this passes my understanding—that, while he encourages priests and monks to enter the state of matrimony and commends it, as

5

one that is holy and well-pleasing to God, yet he, for
his own person, will have none of it.   Even to Albert
of Brandenburg, the Grand Master of the German
Order, he gave the advice: ‘Throw aside the habit of
your order, take a wife, and put a Duke's crown upon
your head,' which the great lord has followed, to the
joy of all believers, and of Luther especially.. It is
known that he urged the Archbishop of Mayence, to
follow the example of his cousin of Prussia.   And does
he not give his friends cause for doubting the earnest-
ness of his teaching, or for fearing that he lacks courage, himself to enter the state which he commends to
others?"

Lucas Kranach nodded assent.   "I think with you,
and I wish with all my heart, that Luther were of another mind in this matter, not only for the sake of his
friends and the good cause, but for his own.   Truly,
if matters continue thus, we shall soon weep behind
his bier; and then, the Lord only knows what will become of the world.   He daily prepares himself for
death, being of the opinion that the work will prosper
without him, it being God's work, who is able to carve
Himself a Dr. Martin out of a willow twig.   But I regard it otherwise, namely, that God will not throw
aside His chosen instruments until his purpose is accomplished, and the world cannot yet forego Luther's

services. But that he may carry out what he has begun, he must not continue alone—without care or service. Even though his bones were of iron, and his
nerves of steel, yet the giant's task, which rests upon
his shoulders, will bear him down, without a faithful
housewife at his side, who will care for the wants of his
body. His spirit is oftentimes so lost in heavenly
matters, as to forget that the body craves rest and
nourishment. Only the other day I found him sitting
in his chair, faint and pale, and at my questioning he
confessed that over the translation of the Psalms, he
had passed two days and two nights without food or
drink. When at night, wearied with the day's work,
he lies down upon his bed, it is a hard one, and no
gentle hand has smoothed his pillow. Oh, that God
would guide his heart to choose a wife who would
be a helpmeet for him! He would soon recover his
strength and be of good courage. But where indeed,"
continued Kranach with a sigh, "where is the woman
worthy of such a man?" He paused, and his eyes
wandered over the crowded square. "See," he exclaimed, "yonder goes your dear wife with Mistress
Katharine! Is it true, as I have been told, that the
Reverend Doctor Caspar Glatz has sued for her hand?"

Reichenbach's face was clouded with annoyance, as
he answered : "You touch upon a matter which trou-

bles me sorely. You doubtless heard that young Baumgaertner, who at one time pursued her with his loving
glances, soon forgot our Kate, and took the wife his
father had chosen for him!   I am almost glad of it,
for Kate now sees that I was in the right, and that the
youth, by reason of his light mind and fickle heart,
was unworthy of her.   But I am distressed at this suit
of Dr. Glatz, which Luther favors, thinking Katharine, as a former nun, most fitted to become the wife
of a God-fearing priest.   He is a good man, and if
the sacrifice must needs be made, I would rather give
her to him than to many another.   But behold, since
Master Nicholas von Amsdorf came at Luther's bid-
ding, to press the Doctor's suit, she is wholly changed.
She heard him in silence, then burst into tears and
said : 'Reverend sir, love cannot be forced or commanded; it must be given by God.   My heart is cold
toward him you bid me marry, and I never could be
to him what a Christian wife should be, according to
God's word and command.   Do not urge me, for I
would rather continue in my present condition all my
life, than give my hand to Dr. Glatz.'   When Amsdorf represented to her that Luther would be ill-pleas-
ed at her refusal, her tears flowed afresh, and she begged that he might not be told; but that she herself
would acquaint him with her decision.   When on that

same day Luther came to us, there was a scene which brought the tears to our eyes. Katharine fell at his feet, and spoke as I have never heard her speak. The Doctor dealt with her as a father with his child, comforted her with gentle, kindly words, and promised not to torment her any further, but to leave the matter in God's hands. After she had gone away, he sat with us for an hour longer, looking very serious, and spoke to us in such moving words, that it was easy to see how greatly he was disturbed by Katharine's trouble. After musing for some moments, he said : '' Now I understand, my friend, why you fear to lose Catharine. She is indeed a treasure, and a maiden after God's own heart. I am vexed with myself, that I have hitherto regarded her so little, when I am really her guardian and her spiritual father.' Since that day Katharine no longer stands timidly aloof from the Doctor, but is ready at all times to speak with him ; and if he commends her housewifely virtues and maidenly reserve, her face beams with pleasure."

Lucas Kranach, who had listened with much attention, replied : '' Yes, Katharine is of an excellent disposition, and grows ever dearer to me. I was heartily glad for her sake, when the exiled King of Denmark, during his recent visit in Wittenberg, gave her a golden ring, in acknowledgment of her womanly virtues.

But God forbid, that such distinction should make her vain ! ''

"Do not fear," Reichenbach replied ; "her mind is not set upon high things.''

In the meantime they had reached the Augustinian monastery, where Luther lived. Two wayfarers, who had doubtless asked help of the Doctor, were coming out of the door ; for no one in Wittenberg was so frequently sought out by the poor and needy, as was the Professor with his salary of 22 thalers and 12 groschen. He gave his last coin, and when that was spent, he did not spare the silver cup, which had been a gift from the Elector.

"Come, let us wish the Doctor a good day," said Kranach. "I desire to thank him for his sermon.''

They crossed the court, and passing through a long, dark passage, reached Luther's cell. They found him sitting at his table—a large pile of letters before him. He received his friends with evident pleasure.

"Welcome, dear friends ! See here—my Sunday-guests, who see to it that Doctor Martin shall have no rest even on this blessed day. They all seem to be wedding-guests. Yes, you may well stare—to-day all my friends would have me marry. Here is a letter from my good friend, Mistress Argula von Grumbach, who with many words urges me to establish by my own

act my doctrine of priestly marriage, and by my own
example to encourage others. Here is another from
Pastor Link in Altenburg. He announces the birth
of a daughter. Here again, my father resumes his old
litany, and speaks with such moving words, that methinks I must reach out after the first maiden I can
find. Now tell me, dear friends, are not these merry
Sunday-guests?"

· Lucas Kranach answered earnestly: "Perhaps they
are God's messengers to you, Martin. Your friends
are in danger of losing faith in your teachings, if you
continue in your present course."

Luther shook his head, where the tonsure had almost disappeared under his curly hair.

"Do my friends so little understand me? See,
dearest Lucas, by what I have said concerning the
sanctity and the necessity of priestly marriage, I will
abide forevermore. For according to God's Word,
there is no condition on earth more blessed than that
of marriage, which God Himself has instituted and
sanctified for men of every degree, and in which state
not only kings and princes and saints, but, although
in a different manner, even the eternal Son of God,
was born. Yet for myself, I have no thought of taking a wife. My enemies are busy enough; for to the
slanders of the Papists are added the revilings of the

'heavenly prophets,' in whose name the ill-condition-
ed Thomas Münzer has published a pamphlet 'against
the ungodly, soft-living flesh at Wittenberg.'   Were I
to marry, they would speedily cry out: 'Aha, now we
see what his Gospel means—to serve the flesh and live
in ease!'   This fear makes even my friends to hesitate,
and Dr. Schurf said but lately: 'If this monk took a
wife, the devils would laugh, and the angels would
weep;' and my dear Philip Melanchthon, who stood
by, added: 'Yes, the Papists are watching for it; and
if he did this thing, he would work his doctrine greater harm than the Pope's excommunication or the Emperor's interdict were able to do.'   Moreover, who
would think of marrying in these troublous times, when
peasants have gone mad, when castles and convents
are burning on all sides, and streams of innocent blood
are flowing?   Nor do I experience within myself the
least inclination thereto.   I am indeed in the Lord's
hand, who can turn my heart and mind whenever it
pleases Him.   But as I am now disposed, I will not
take a wife.   Not that I am of wood or stone, but my
mind is averse to marriage, and I daily anticipate a
heretic's doom.   Nor would I harden my heart, or
reason with the Lord—but I trust that He will not suffer me to abide much longer in this world.   Finally,
when I advocated the marriage of priests, I did not

thereby intend to impose a new sort of bondage, or to place a new yoke upon men's necks, like the unhappy Karlstadt, who would perforce compel every priest to marry. There shall be perfect liberty in this matter —either to do, or to leave undone."

Luther spoke in a tone of such very decided conviction, that Kranach did not venture to reply. He grasped the Doctor's hand, asking his friend's pardon with his eyes. Reichenbach also arose, and said gently: "God will provide!"

The two men took their leave, and Luther, being much wearied, called Wolfgang, and bade him read aloud to him the remaining letters.

CHAPTER VIII.

A SUDDEN RESOLVE.

NEW YEAR'S DAY of 1525 was a gloomy one, full of premonitions of coming evil. Even darker and heavier rose the storm-clouds, which had been gathering since October. In Thuringia, in Franconia and Suabia, disturbances had arisen among the oppressed peasantry—when Luther's "Sermon on Christian Liberty" fell like a spark among the explosive material, kindling a flame that startled the world. Luther, in whom the wretched peasants put their trust, had earnestly advocated their cause, and with a prophetic voice appealed to the consciences of the nobles; urging them to grant the just demands of the peasants, as set forth in their twelve articles. Peace would no doubt have speedily followed, had the knights consented to reason or mercy. But when they gave no heed to Luther's warning, and stubbornly persisted in their cruel exactions, the storm burst. Like an avalanche, gathering strength at every step, the rebellion, beginning in the Black Forest, spread over Suabia, Thuringia and Franconia. On all sides castles and convents

(74)

stood in flames, and the blood of the murdered ones cried aloud to Heaven. Instigated by the "prophets" of Zwickau, the peasants were seized with a wild bestial frenzy, and a deadly terror paralyzed the hands of princes and nobles.

Luther was deeply grieved. With his fearless heroism, he twice ventured among the raging mob, endeavoring to recall them to their senses. But for once his voice was powerless. With a heavy heart he returned to Wittenberg, and with a heart still heavier, he wrote his pamphlet "against the plundering and murderous peasants," calling upon the princes to draw the sword in defence of their own. By degrees they collected their forces, and met the disorderly bands with experienced and disciplined troops. The insurgents succumbed; but, to his sorrow, Luther saw the victors wreaking unworthy vengeance upon all who wore the peasant's smock.

The church-bells throughout the land proclaimed the return of peace, and all hearts shared in the general thanksgiving. But Luther sat in his cell, and mourned. He bowed his head, refusing food and drink—for every man's hand was against him. The Papists showered curses and imprecations upon his head: "Thou art the man whose blasphemous words concerning Christian liberty, broke the fetters of the peasants, and caused this bloodshed." The peasants in their turn cried out: "Thou hast deceived our hopes, hast betrayed and forsaken us!" His friends scarcely ventured to show themselves. And the Gospel? Ah·! it seemed as though all were at an end!

That the measure of his misery might be full, the crushing news came from Torgau, that the prince, whose wisdom and firmness had been a strong defence and support of the Gospel, had, on the 5th of May, departed from this evil world. Was night again to cover the earth, after the morning star of the Gospel had risen so brightly in the Heavens? Would God cast away his servant—his faithful servant, who, like a conquering hero, had begun his course so gloriously?

In Wittenberg there was much anxious questioning. Where was Luther? His pulpit was silent. His chair at the University was empty. He was sitting alone in his cell, lost to outward affairs, and wholly absorbed in the inner world of thought and prayer. It was always thus on the eve of a great resolution. Thus he had sat and meditated, when he was wrestling with the resolve, in defiance of the pope and the whole world, to speak the truth, and to begin the struggle with the superstitions of Rome.

Does he utter Elijah's complaint: "It is enough; now, O Lord, take away my life!" Does he despair

of himself, and of his mission? No—but a fierce, heroic struggle is passing in his soul. At last he is able
to pray; and the bruised spirit finds the open door,
from whence cometh its help. The heavy eyes flash
with a new fire; the furrowed brow grows clear; his
upturned face breathes a holy defiance. Suddenly he
leaves his cell and repairs to the house of Lucas Kranach, one of his dearest friends.

The artist was standing at his easel, engaged upon
a portrait of Bugenhagen, the preacher of the town-
church. At Luther's entrance, he dropped his brush
and received his friend with open arms.

"My Martin! Thank God that I see you again!
We were in sore trouble on your behalf. But what
great thing has happened, Martin? Your face shines
as it does when some great thought has taken possession of you."

Luther met his friend's eyes with a solemn gaze:
"Send for Dr. Bugenhagen, and for the lawyer, Dr.
Apel—I desire to ask a friendly service of you three."

Kranach sent a messenger to the two men, who soon
arrived, and rejoiced no less than the painter, at the
sight of their friend.

Luther began: "My dear friends, a change has
come over me, which will cause you to marvel greatly.
Not to keep you in suspense, I will tell you at once:

Brother Martin has received the Lord's command to take to himself a wife ! "

In mute surprise all eyes were fixed upon Luther, who calmly continued : " It is the Lord's doing, and little short of a miracle in my own eyes. Therefore my heart consents willingly."

" The Lord's Name be praised," cried Lucas Kranach, who was the first to recover from his astonishment. " Brother Martin, this is indeed from God, and an answer to my secret prayers. But tell us whom, among the daughters of the land, have you chosen ? "

" Her name is Katharine von Bora," answered Luther.

Again there was a silence ; then the three men, with one accord, hastened to their friend, and warmly pressed his hands. " This also is from God," exclaimed Kranach, " for among all the maidens of my acquaintance, she is the most worthy."

Bugenhagen, in hearty, earnest words expressed his pleasure at Luther's choice, while Kranach hurried from the room, and soon returned with his wife.

In Mistress Barbara's eyes two great tears were glistening, as she offered her hand to Luther. " Blessings upon you, reverend Doctor," she said with a trembling voice, " and blessed is the maiden of your choice. How I thank the dear Lord, who has thus shown you His mercy, after the afflictions of these times. Ah, Doctor, heretofore you have, in high and noble words, lauded the holy state of matrimony, but you will find in this blessed condition more than words can tell."

A servant brought a flagon of wine and four silver cups on a golden salver.

"Be seated, dear friends," urged Kranach, while Mistress Barbara filled the cups with sparkling Spanish wine.

"Now tell us, Brother Martin," said Kranach, rubbing his hands with glee, "how did this change come to pass? For I no longer dared hope for such a resolution from you."

Luther took a draught of the wine and answered : "Man proposes and God disposes; and when He drives the human heart, it is hard to kick against the pricks. I considered three things ; first, my enemies, who are waxing ever bolder and more malicious, and accuse me of driving others whither I myself fear to follow. Therefore, in defiance of the Devil, the princes and bishops, I will take a wife, thus testifying to the holiness of marriage, which they despise and reject. I will not delay, that I may still have time to enforce my doctrine by my own act. The times are

evil, and my last hour may be near at hand, and I
would that death should find me wedded.   Then, I
considered my old father.   I called to mind my grief
when, as a disobedient son, I entered the monastery.
I would fain repair my wrong-doing, and say to him
some day, in answer to his pleadings: 'See, dear father, Martin has a wife.   Be at rest, and rejoice with
him!'   In the third place, I considered my friends,
whose courage is weak, and who fear to marry, while
Luther remains single.   Thus would I, by my own example, establish the doctrine I have preached."

"Dear Kate," exclaimed Mistress Barbara, with enthusiasm, "Blessed art thou among women; the lines
are fallen unto thee in pleasant places!"

"Does she know what is in store for her?" asked
Dr. Apel.

Luther replied: "I have seen her more frequently
of late, and I observed with pleasure, how her inner
worth, her housewifely virtues, and her noble mind
were more and more clearly revealed to me.   Yet I
am not an ardent lover.   I am past forty, and my
heart beats calmly, although I love her well.   Therefore she doubtless has no suspicion of my purpose; but
I trust that she will not refuse me her hand.   I would
request you, my friends, to accompany me, that my
betrothal, made before witnesses, may have force and

validity in the world's eyes."

" This is a joyous errand ; few such have fallen to my lot," said Kranach. " But tell me, Martin, why will you carry out your purpose thus secretly ? Melanchthon—"

" Do not speak to me of him," interrupted Luther, " he is of a timid nature—he and others of my friends, who fear that my work will fall to pieces if I take a wife, especially one who was once a nun. What is to be done, must be done quickly, lest the Devil cause confusion by the evil speaking of friends as well as foes."

Dr. Apel seemed lost in thought. Suddenly he lifted his head, and with an embarrassed smile, turned to Luther, " I rejoice at this with all my heart. But I have some misgiving, whether Katharine, with all the excellence of her heart and disposition, is suited to you, and will continue to satisfy you. For I fear she has brought but little knowledge or learning with her from the convent. Forgive me for thus speaking my thought."

Luther's eyes shone. " My dear Apel, tell me, what is it that makes Melanchthon's wife so dear to him, and his house the abode of happiness ? He did not seek after a learned wife, but looked to the heart alone. A learned woman is no better than a gadfly,

6

that glitters and yet stings. The woman who pleases her husband, and makes marriage a paradise on earth, is one with a gentle, God-fearing heart, loving and faithful, with a firm and skilful hand to govern her household.''

A grateful glance from Barbara's eyes thanked him for his words.

"Now let us go, in God's Name," said Kranach, reaching for his cloak and hat.

They left the house, and Barbara silently made the sign of the holy cross after them.''

.   .   .   .

Mistress Riechenbach and Katharine von Bora were sitting together in the great hall, preparing vegetables for the family dinner.

"Is it true," asked the latter, "that the new elector has promised to give his earnest support to the Gospel?"

Elsa assented. "During the lifetime of his brother, of blessed memory, he frequently expressed his devotion to the Gospel, and has always shown much respect to Dr. Martin.

Katharine's eyes flashed. "Honor to whom honor is due. The Doctor is greater than any—the Emperor, kings and princes must do him homage.''

Mistress Elsa smiled at the enthusiasm which every mention of Luther's name called forth in Katharine, and changed the conversation. .

Suddenly a loud knock was heard. Katharine hastened to open the door, and Luther, Kranach, Bugenhagen, and Apel entered. Their greeting was so formal and solemn, that Katharine stepped aside in surprise.

They approached Mistress Elsa, whom the strange solemnity of their appearance had put in a flutter of embarrassment.

"Will you permit me," said Luther, "in the presence of yourself, and of these three honorable men, to speak with Katharine von Bora, upon a matter of great moment?"

Questioning with her eyes first Luther, then the others, who had remained in the background, Mistress Elsa, after a slight hesitation, called to Katharine, who approached with a feeling of uneasy apprehension.

"Dear Mistress Kate," Luther began, "you know how great is my interest in your welfare, and how I have endeavored to find for you a worthy husband, that as a wife you might fulfil your true vocation. But to this day my efforts have been unavailing, whereat I have been much troubled. But the proverb says: Of all good things there are three—therefore I again come to you in a matter of this nature, and entreat you—''

Her hands were lifted with a gesture of dismay.

"Do not fear, dear Katharine," continued Luther, in a gentle tone. "To-day I appear not for another, but, since God has put it into my heart, to delay no longer in enforcing my teaching by my example, and it has told me, without questioning, who was its choice, therefore I ask you, in the presence of God and these human witnesses, whether you will plight your troth to Dr. Martin Luther, and be his wedded wife?''

A deep silence succeeded. The three men stood immovable. Mistress Elsa stared at the Doctor with wide-open eyes. And Katharine? Her frame trembled; she caught the arm of a chair for support. Her face was pale, and her heart seemed to have stopped its beating.

Suddenly she lifted her clasped hands and whispered in happy forgetfulness of her surroundings: "Lord, my God, Thou knowest that I would have esteemed it happiness to be his servant! and now I am held worthy to be his wife! Lord, Thy mercy is very great!''

From Mistress Elsa's side of the room loud sobs were heard. Deeply moved, Luther took Katharine's hand.

"Then you will be mine until death?''

"Yes," came the happy, trembling answer, her

heart sending back the rosy color to her cheeks. Never in her life had she seemed so fair, as in this moment of her supreme happiness.

Then the "great Doctor" sealed his betrothal with a kiss.

. . . .

Light streamed from the upper windows of Master Reichenbach's house on the evening of this eventful day. A festive company was gathered in the splendid apartments. Before an altar, bright with flowers and lights, knelt Martin Luther and Katharine von Bora, surrounded by their friends, who reverently, with folded hands, listened as Luther prayed: "Dear heavenly Father, who hast vouchsafed to bestow upon me Thy fatherly name and office, grant me grace and blessing to rule and govern my wife and household in Thy fear. Give unto me wisdom and strength, and unto them a willing heart and mind, to follow and obey Thy Commandments, through Jesus Christ. Amen."

"Amen," responded the others, and Bugenhagen placed the rings on the hands of the betrothed pair, blessing their union in the name of the holy Trinity.

This was done on Tuesday after the feast of the Holy Trinity, the 13th of June, 1525.

CHAPTER IX.

A DAY OF REJOICING.

THE rooks who lodged among the grey walls of the Augustinian Convent at Wittenberg, peeped curiously forth from their nests, to discover the cause of the unwonted activity throughout the silent house. They were accustomed to being left in undisputed possession, but now they fluttered about in dismay, as many people, busily going and coming, carried in all manner of household goods, such as seemed to them ill-suited to a convent. Still greater was their surprise, when the kind monk, who had daily thrown them a few handfuls of grain, no longer showed himself, and they were forced to fly abroad for their daily bread.

A bustling activity had now entered the lonely old house. With busy haste, Frau Elsa went in and out. The large room, overlooking the court, was being freshly painted under her directions, and supplied with costly furniture. She came each day to feast her eyes upon the pleasant home she was preparing for her beloved Kate. But she kept the door carefully locked

(86)

and the key hidden in her pocket—for Kate was to
know nothing of this until the day when Luther would
bring his bride to his home—which was to be on the
27th of June.

As the day drew near, the commotion increased,
and Frau Elsa saw with heartfelt joy, how persons of
all degrees sought to testify to Dr. Martin their love
and devotion. Her eyes filled with tears, when one
day an aged peasant woman came hobbling in on her
crutch. She brought in a basket a hen and six little
chicks, saying that she must give something to the
man who, like the Saviour of old, had restored to a
a widowed mother her only son; for at Luther's word
the convent gates had opened, and her son had come
back to her.

Many others came, with stores for the kitchen and
larder, and Frau Elsa could scarcely find room for so
many provisions. Shortly before the appointed day,
the Senate of Wittenberg sent as a token of its esteem,
a barrel of Eimbeck beer, and twenty gold florins for
the Doctor—and for Mistress Katharine a piece of fine
Suabian linen, together with the written promise, to
supply the newly wedded couple for one year with table wine.

On the following day the University of Wittenberg
sent to the greatest of its teachers a huge silver tank-

kard, lined with gold, and richly chased. The inscription reads thus: " The honorable University of the City of Wittenberg sends this bridal gift to Dr. Martin Luther and Katharine von Bora; in the year 1525, on Tuesday after the Feast of St. John the Baptist."

Frau Elsa was busily arranging the many wedding gifts about the room. With a smile she said to herself: "What will the Doctor say to these tokens of affection, after he had strictly forbidden all gifts from his friends," when a wagon rolled into the court, and the Elector's serving men unloaded a large wild boar and two roebucks. They charged the wondering Elsa with a greeting from the court-preacher, Spalatin, to Dr. Luther, and in the confusion of her happiness, she had well nigh embraced the bearer of the message.

Meanwhile, Luther sat in his cell, writing the last of his wedding invitations. A number of letters had already been dispatched to more distant friends—to his aged parents at Mansfeld, to the three Senators of that town, to his friends in Altenburg—Spalatin and Link, and to Amsdorf and others, in Magdeburg. This last one had almost been forgotten, although it should have been the first, being directed to the merchant, Leonhard Koppe, in Torgau, without whose deed of mercy, Luther had doubtless never seen his Kate.

"Dear and reverend Father Prior," it ran, "you know what has befallen? namely, that the nun, whom two years ago you rescued from one convent, is about to enter another—not however to take the veil, but to become the housewife of Dr. Luther, who heretofore has dwelt alone in the old, forsaken Augustinian monastery in Wittenberg. God delights in preparing surprises, both for me and for the world. I pray you, therefore, to come to my wedding on the Tuesday after the feast of St. John the Baptist—but without gifts."

The important day had arrived. All Wittenberg was in a flutter of festive excitement, and many fervent prayers ascended heavenward. In the convent a distinguished company sat at table with Dr. Martin, at whose side Katharine, in wordless bliss, heard what the guests had to say in praise of the newly-wedded pair.

She was as one in a dream. She felt as though she were lifted from the condition of a servant to that of a queen, for he who sat beside her was a king indeed in the realms of thought ; his sovereignty being attested alike by the praise of his friends and by the deadly hatred of his foes. And she, the humble maiden, was henceforth to stand nearer to this great man, than the most intimate of his friends—nearer than Melanch-

thon, or Kranach, than Bugenhagen or Jonas. She
pressed her hand to her heart to still its beating, and
the prayer rose from her soul: "Lord, help me, lest I
grow proud.   Keep me humble always."

Notwithstanding the happiness which beamed from
Luther's face, a certain restlessness was perceptible in
his manner, and he whispered to Katharine: "Now I
shall hope no longer.   God has seen fit to deny me
this wish, lest there be too much of joy."   Katharine
understood.

Suddenly the student, John Pfister, who acted as
cup bearer, announced that an aged couple stood without, who desired to see Dr. Martin.   Luther ordered
them to be brought in, and presently two old people,
in the dress of the Mansfeld peasants, appeared at the
door, where they paused, as if startled at the sight of so
large a company.

Luther had risen from his seat, and as he hastened
toward them, the old woman stretched out her arms,
and cried : "My son Martin !"

She sank upon her son's breast and wept aloud.
Luther disengaged himself for a moment, to greet his
father: "Dearest father, you are a thousand times
welcome !   I have heartily desired to know, whether
you have forgiven your disobedient son.   God has led
me by wondrous ways, and we must bless His name,

for whatsoever He begins, He carries out most gloriously."

He turned, and pointing to Katharine, who had come nearer, said : "Father, this is your daughter."

The old man trembled, and lifting his clasped hands he exclaimed, "Now I will gladly die, since my eyes have seen this day. Martin, you are again my son indeed, and old Hans Luther is a happy father."

The wedding guests surrounded the old people, to whom the place of honor beside the bridal pair was assigned, and Dr. Martin said :

"My happiness is now complete. I had asked this one thing of the Lord, that to-day I might see my dear parents face to face, and he has heard my prayer. This I accept as a special token of his favor, and will thank Him therefor as long as I live."

BOOK SECOND.

KATHARINE VON BORA;

THE WIFE.

(93)

THE WIFE.

CHAPTER X.

"AS SORROWING, YET ALWAYS REJOICING."

IT was the season, when summer gives place to autumn ; when the evenings grow long, and the lamps are lighted early.

In his study, Dr. Martin was seated at his great oaken table busily writing. A hanging lamp shed a pleasant light, and the stove of green tiles diffused a cheerful warmth. A brown spaniel lay curled up on the floor. On the wall near the book-shelves hung a handsome clock in a tall, slender case of polished cedarwood, whose long pendulum gravely measured the seconds. It had been a bridal gift from the Protestant Abbot Frederick, of Nuremberg.

Beside her husband sat Katharine with her spinning wheel. She was dressed in a simple gown of black woollen stuff, and her hair was hidden under a white coif. From time to time her eyes turned with a loving, reverent glance toward her husband. The silence was unbroken, save by the scratching of Luther's pen, the humming of Katharine's wheel, and the crackling of the fire.

Suddenly the spindle slipped and fell to the floor with a crash, which startled the Doctor out of his meditations. Katharine rose in dismay. "Do not be angry, dearest Doctor, I will go elsewhere, lest my carelessness disturb you."

Luther looked up. "Not so, dear Kate. Have I not often told you that your presence is not a hindrance, but rather a help to me? I once imagined that a man who was unencumbered by a wife and by the cares of a household, could work with more profit. But I have learned to think differently. It seems as though my thoughts were freer, and my pen more ready, when you are near me. Every day I thank my God for the good and faithful wife He has given me. As I expected, my enemies make more noise than ever, and I am a worse heretic, in consequence of my marriage, than when I touched the pope's crown and the monks' soft living. But I am of good cheer nevertheless. For if my marriage is God's work, small wonder that the world is offended at it. Is it not an offence to the world, that the Creator gave His life as a ransom for mankind? If the world were my friend, I should fear that my work was not of God."

Katharine listened with increasing delight. "Ah, dearest Doctor, your speech makes my heart glad. When the evil-speakers attacked me, they caused me many a sleepless night. But my sorrow was ten times greater, when you for my sake experienced an increase of enmity. When you tell me that you rejoice at the world's displeasure, I too am comforted. If our enemies had eyes to see, they would cease to speak evil of us, and rather envy the calm and peaceful happiness which marriage has brought us."

Luther laid down his pen and said: "Yes, dear wife, you speak truly. Marriage is a holy place, with an altar, upon which incense is continually burning. All the troubles of life grow light, when each bears the other's burdens. I have a pious, faithful wife, to whom I may safely entrust all I have, even my own life. And you, Kate, have a God-fearing husband, who loves you, and esteems you more highly, than the kingdom of France, or the principality of Venice."

With a blush Katharine asked, as she bent over the table: "What are you writing, Doctor?"

Luther took up a sheet of paper: "See," he said, "these words are blows designed for a crowned head, —that of King Henry of England. Do not be alarmed, dear Kate,—Dr. Martin, whom he calls a "mangy dog" and a "hellish wolf," will tell him what will

7

subdue his lofty spirit.   I had well-nigh forgotten what he wrote against me in 1521, and silence would have been the fittest answer to such unkingly language ; but when, on the occasion of my marriage, he renewed his attacks in vile words, I could no longer keep silence. Would you hear what I have written ?"

As Katharine seemed eager to hear, he read aloud to her the first pages of his manuscript.

She seemed much pleased. "Ah, Doctor, how softly you tread ! This pleases me well, and I would beg of you in future also to restrain your anger, for with calmness and deliberation one can deal more telling blows, than with hasty words—and perhaps in the end win the enemy's good-will."

With a smile, the Doctor took his wife's hand. "I thank you for such words. Although a woman's duty does not lie in meddling with her husband's business, yet a man suffers no harm, if his wife exhorts him to peace and gentleness, and by her example induces him to make these virtues his own. I confess that I have often yielded to my anger, and have poured oil upon the flames, when perhaps with moderation and patience I might have quenched the fire. In this matter you shall be my taskmaster, and I will thank God for the faithful friend he has given me in you."

Voices were heard outside, and presently Dorothy, the maid-servant, entered with a roll of paper. "A messenger stands without, who charged me to deliver this into Dr. Luther's hands."

Luther opened the roll and found therein letters from two Leipsic theologians—a Latin address to himself, from Master Joachim von der Heyden, and a German one to Katharine, signed by Master John Hasenberg, otherwise Myricianus.

"See here," laughed Luther, "Katharine Luther has become a famous woman, since learned writings are addressed to her!"

With mock solemnity he placed one of the papers in her hand. But he laughed no more, when he read the one directed to himself, and Katharine's face paled and flushed by turns, as she acquainted herself with the contents of the other. She was unable to finish. It seemed as though her heart must stop its beating, when Martin Luther, the object of her deepest veneration, was assailed in foul language, and the advice was given her, to flee from his unholy presence, and return to the heavenly Bridegroom, with whom she had broken her faith. With pain and dread her eyes sought her husband's face, where a dark cloud was gathering, as he waded through a flood of abuse and slander. But the cloud soon disappeared, and the old, cheerful calm took its place, as with a merry laugh he flung the letter on the table.   Then he turned to Katharine and said : "What have they written you, my dear wife ?   I doubt not they have served you with the same dainty repast.   Shall we follow their advice, take our staff, and return at once to the bosom of the all-saving church ? "

With a sad smile Katharine replied : " How can you jest ?   My heart is sorely troubled."

" Not so, dear Kate," Luther comforted her ; "I am of good cheer ; for the more furiously the enemies rage and threaten, the more blessed seems the lot which God has granted me, and all their malice only serves to show me the more clearly the holiness of marriage."

Here Wolfgang entered, and reported that the messenger was still waiting for his fee.   Luther quickly thrust his hand into his pocket, and finding it empty, he unlocked a cabinet, and took out two golden florins.

" Truly, the man must needs have a rich reward, for helping me to such joy and contentment.   Bring him in."

When the man appeared, Luther tapped him on the shoulder and said kindly : " Dear friend, go home in peace, and tell those who sent you, that their letters have caused us much pleasure. You, as the bearer, take these two florins as your reward, together with the blessing of Dr. Martin and of Mistress Katharine, his wife."

The man, in great embarrassment, was uncertain whether Luther were in jest or in earnest, and hesitated to accept the rich gift. But Luther's manner was irresistible, and with his friendly wishes for a safe journey, the messenger took his departure. Then Luther turned to Katharine, who was still struggling with her feelings. "See, dear Kate, the Devil and the world would fain have you leave Dr. Martin. But the harder they press you, the more firmly I shall hold you; for here alone is your abiding-place."

Softly weeping, Katharine rested her head upon his breast. But her tears were no longer tears of sadness.

CHAPTER XI

THE FAITHFUL ECKART.

"WHERE may Hans be staying? I hope he has not repented of his purpose!"

"Never fear, Eberhard, for it was he whose rage was fiercest against the last scoundrelly act of the heretic! Landlord, fill my cup!"

"And mine," cried a third voice.

When the landlord had brought the wine, a young nobleman clattered into the room, much excited, and was received by his friends with a noisy welcome.

They were in an inn near Wurtzen, that bore the sign of "the blue pike." A dim torch sputtered in the close, low room, and threw flickering lights upon the faces of the four men. Everything in the room was unclean; the landlord himself, with his dirt-stained jacket and grimy face, seemed a sworn foe to soap and water. It was doubtless long since he had entertained such noble guests, who seemed ill at ease in the filthy den.

They were four young squires from the neighborhood, Hans von Soldau, Eberhard von Kriebitsch,

(102)

Wolf von Steinbach, and Joachim von Spergau, who
had appointed this secret meeting at the "blue
pike."

" It is well that you come, Hans," cried one of them
to the belated conspirator, while the landlord received an unmistakable hint to betake himself elsewhere.

" Do not be angry, friends, that I come thus late,"
croaked Hans von Soldau in a hoarse voice, as he
seated himself. "I desired to make some further in-
quiries ; for a rumor came to my ears, that fortune was
favoring our design, and would shortly provide a convenient opportunity for our revenge."

" What is it?" exclaimed the others, starting from
their seats.

Hans lifted both hands. " Be quiet, and hear me.
I first went to the priest and made confession of my
purpose, that I might be able with greater courage and
confidence to put my hand to the work. The reverend father gave me his blessing, and promised me an
abundant reward in Heaven. Yet he disapproves of
open violence, lest we kindle a fresh fire, more dangerous than the peasants' war. We must act secretly,
that none may know what has become of the heretic."
He rose, and in a louder tone continued : " Friends,
brothers ! We are in the same position and must therefore hold together. Each one of us has seen his patri-

mony lessened by the unwelcome return of a sister.
Was it for this we urged our parents to place them in
convents, that this infamous monk should open the
doors for their escape? Woe be to you, Luther! At
Nimptschen you succeeded, but it was to your own
undoing that you stretched forth your ruthless hand
toward Freiberg.''

In a fierce rage, Wolf von Steinbach struck upon the
table and roared : "I am poorer by ten thousand florins!   Luther, it is you whom I shall pay for it!''

"I would gladly forego the beggarly inheritance,''
growled Eberhard von Kriebitsch, with an angry
frown, " but I refuse to harbor that dragon, my step-
sister, with whom I have quarreled since the days of
my childhood!''

"Calm yourselves,'' urged Joachim von Spergau,
" and let us learn what is the opportunity which fortune throws into our way.''

Hans von Soldau drew his fingers through his flowing red beard, and related: "The Elector's court
chaplain and private secretary, Spalatin, intends to be
married on the 19th of November, and has invited Luther to his wedding. About two hours ago, I acci-
dentally met the messenger bearing Luther's answer to
Altenburg. Tell me, friends, does not everything
shape itself to our advantage. Ha, Luther, your last

bread will soon be baked ! "

A deep silence followed his words. Hans stared fiercely at the conspirators, and exclaimed: "Cowards ! does your heart fail you ! Then I shall venture alone."

Joachim von Spergau, the most cautious of the band, replied in an injured tone : " Do not question our hon‧ or, Hans ! It is not cowardise, if we hesitate for a moment, before we consent to a deed of blood."

"It may possibly be accomplished without bloodshed," explained Hans, in a milder tone. "My confessor knows a place where the heretic need not die, and yet will be dead to the world. If it should become necessary to dispatch him, you must now solemnly declare, whether you will lend a hand. If you shrink from the sight of blood, then go your way, and I alone will have the glory of ridding the world of this pestilent fellow. If you are minded to stand by me, lift up your hands, and swear."

It evidently cost the others a violent effort, to bind themselves by an oath to a probable murder ; for this idea had not been entertained from the beginning. But the reproachful scorn, which flashed from Hans' eyes, drove them to a hasty resolve, and they took the oath.

After the young squires had arranged the details of

the attack, they paid their reckoning, and mounting
their horses, disappeared in the darkness.

.   .   .   .

"Why are you so sad, dear Kate?" Luther asked
his wife one day; "have you any trouble of body or
mind, that you are hiding from me?"

Katharine sighed.   "A heavy weight lies upon my
heart, and I know not what it means.   There are forebodings, which one cannot explain, and yet they will
not be driven away."

"And what is your foreboding?" asked Luther with
a smile.

"I fear that some great misfortune is awaiting us."

Luther lifted his finger warningly: "You see ghosts
where none exist.   Do you not know, that such seeing
is harmful—troubling our own heart, and also displea-
sing the Lord God?   We should fear no evil, when
God's angels are watching over us.   Methinks your
trouble is nothing more than the added burden of ca-
ring for the three noble nuns, who have sought refuge
with us.   Do not let this fret you, nor grudge to the
poor fugitives the shelter of our house, until the anger
of their people is appeased."

"You do me injustice, dear Doctor," interrupted
Katharine.   "I received them willingly, much rather

than the five monks from Thuringia, to whom, besides food and drink, you gave cloth for new jackets, and who afterwards broke into our house as thieves. No, dear Doctor, our nuns from Freiberg are most dear to me, and I will gladly share with them what I have,— and moreover the Elector yesterday sent a fresh load of corn, malt and wood. Yet their presence does cause me some uneasiness, especially that of the duchess Ursala von Münsterberg—who, being the niece of Duke George, your enemy, may indeed bring danger to our house."

"Be quiet, dear Kate," said Luther, and commit yourself into the Lord's hands. What we are doing toward these unhappy women is a good deed, and well-pleasing to God, who will not permit us to come to harm for their sakes. If, nevertheless, we should suffer for this, remember that it is written : 'Blessed are ye, when men shall revile you and persecute you, for my sake.'"

Kate was silent, and tried to banish her troublesome thoughts, but her heart still refused to be silenced.

On the following morning, after the morning prayer, when the guests and servants had left the room, Katharine came to her husband with a serious face. "Dearest Doctor,—I have learned the cause of my

fear.   The Lord revealed it to me last night in dream.
What is your opinion of dreams?"

Luther replied: "The Scripture teaches us, that
God has at various times made use of dreams, to reveal
to men His thoughts, and to show them the things of
the future, either for their instruction or warning.
What was your dream?"

"I saw you," answered Kate, "journeying in an
open wagon to Altenburg, whither you were going to
attend the wedding of your friend Spalatin.   On the
road, four men in armor sprang from an ambush, dragged you from the wagon, and struck at your head with
their swords, that the blood gushed forth.   Ursula von
Münsterberg, the nun, stood by and tore her hair.
When I awoke, I was glad to find it but a dream.   But
when I slept again, behold, the dream returned, and
showed me the same picture.   Then I perceived that
it was no delusion, but a warning from God, not to go
upon this journey.   Dear Doctor, I beg of you, for
Christ's sake, stay at home—for if you go, I shall be
consumed with fear for your safety."

She clung to her husband's arm and looked at him
with eyes full of piteous entreaty.   Although her
dreaming was little to his taste, yet he was moved by
her distress.   With a glance of tender love, he said
gently: "I am sorry for my friend Spalatin, who will

be unwilling to forego my presence on the great day ; but I should be still more sorry for you, dear wife, if you were troubling yourself here at home, while I made merry in Altenburg. I will write to Spalatin, not to expect me.''

Followed by a grateful look from Katharine, Luther went to his study, and wrote his letter, which ran thus :

'' My Spalatin ! Gladly would I come to your wedding and rejoice with you and yours, were it not that an obstacle has arisen in the way, which I am unable to remove—namely, the tears of my Kate, who imagines that you ask of me nothing less, than to imperil my life. Her loving heart, warned by a two-fold dream, foresees danger to me, as though murderers were lying in wait for me on the road. It does not seem altogether improbable, it having come to my knowledge, that the recent escape of the nuns from the convent at Freiberg, has greatly incensed the nobles in Duke George's land. Although I know that I am everywhere in the hands of the Almighty, and that not a hair of my head can suffer harm, unless it be His will, yet my heart is moved to pity for my poor Kate, who would grieve herself half to death in my absence. You will therefore not be offended, if I am unable to

be present at your marriage, upon which I invoke
God's richest blessing and peace.

MARTIN LUTHER."

"Wittenberg, on St. Martin's Day,
    November 11th 1525."

The messenger who was to carry the letter to Altenburg, received from Katharine an additional fee, and
a flask of Frankish wine for his refreshment on the
way.   When she saw him disappear through the court
yard gate, she breathed a deep sigh of relief, and a
fervent, upturned glance bore her thanksgiving to the
throne of God.

Scarcely a fortnight had passed, when Luther received from Spalatin the following letter :

"My dear Brother Martin :—Although I greatly regretted your absence on the day of my marriage, since
your society is more precious to me than any other,
yet now I rejoice, seeing that God's hand has inter-
posed to preserve you from a great danger. It has
been discovered, that four noblemen were lying in
ambush, intending to make an end of you—since, in
freeing their sisters from the convent, you have caused
them temporal loss, inasmuch as it is now necessary to
make provision for the maidens. One of them especially, Hans von Soldau, is a fierce, lawless fellow, from
whom any evil deed may be expected. Thank your

dear Kate, dear friend, for under God's guidance she has proved your faithful Eckart.

"God's grace be with you!   SPALATIN."

Deeply moved, Luther laid down the letter, and sought his wife, who was busy in the kitchen. To her surprise, he folded her in his arms, and kissing her on both cheeks, said tenderly : "My faithful Eckart."

CHAPTER XII.

A NEW LIFE.

"SEE, Wolfgang, how lustily our garden things are growing," said Luther one sunny afternoon in June of 1526 to his amanuensis, the lame Wolfgang Sieberger, who came limping after him. "Here are the onions and radishes grown from seed my friend Langen sent me, and yonder the melons and cucumbers from Wenzel Link in Nuremberg. The roses from Altenburg please me much; the buds are ready to burst. How delighted Mistress Kate will be, when I bring her the first of our roses. But, Wolfgang, how comes it that your jacket is so soiled? Have you been at work in the stable? Save your reputation, my learned famulus!"

Wolfgang brushed the straw from his sleeve, and answered with an important look: "Had I not helped we would be poorer by one sucking pig, which in its youthful frivolity wandered away and fell into a ditch."

Luther laughed heartily: "Dr. Martin has indeed become a farmer, Mistress Kate a farmer's wife, and

Master Wolfgang a farm-servant. I never dreamed that such honor and dignity would befall me. When I return from my pulpit or lecture-hall, and enter the court, where in former times a solemn silence reigned, I am greeted on all sides by such a cackling and grunting and bleating, that my heart fails me, when I think of all the pious monks and abbots, who are sleeping their last sleep here below. What would they say to such deafening noises in this sacred spot? If I would walk in the garden, and enjoy the fragrance of the flowers, suddenly a swarm of bees flies buzzing about my head, and I have learned, to my sorrow, how sharp a sword they carry. The convent is alive with human beings— almost too many, methinks. In the end it will be needful that I buy a horse of Abraham the Jew, and myself follow the plough.''

Wolfgang listened with a smile and shook his head : '' Reverend Doctor, you jest about the busy life in your house, and yet you owe thanks to those who have brought it about ; for without it, you would fare ill, and so forth.''

'' What do you mean, Wolf? '' asked Luther.

'' What do I mean? '' said Wolfgang, limping a few steps nearer. '' My meaning can be made clear to you without figures, and so forth. What is the amount of the salary paid you by the Elect or since your mar-

8

riage? Two hundred florins. How much have we spent during the past year? Nearly five hundred florins, including the three silver drinking cups."

"Wolf," exclaimed Luther, "that is a strange reckoning."

"It is correct," continued Wolfgang, with growing excitement, "for according to your directions I have kept the books, and so forth. If you will remember, how many guests have sat at your table during the year, how many poor students have been fed daily, how many monks, and nuns, and others, have eaten of your substance, not to mention the gifts which your boundless generosity has scattered with open hands— if you will take this into consideration, and so forth, you will perceive that two hundred florins cannot last the year. Your purse is ever open, and everybody's hand is in it. Truly, you had been a beggar, and in a debtor's prison, and so forth, had not Mistress Luther managed so wisely, and had she not been careful to turn everything to profit, and so forth. I regard the Mistress with deep reverence, for with all her gentleness she has a clear and courageous spirit, and although so many burdens rest upon her, she never grows weary, but has at all times a cheerful heart, and guides her household with a firm and skillful hand, and so forth. But all this farm-yard business would not be needed, if the reverend Doctor would but consent to receive pay for his services to the University. Still larger sums would you gather, if you accepted what the printers offer for your books, and especially for the translation of the Holy Scriptures. You would soon be a veritable Crœsus, and relieved of all care concerning temporal things.''

Luther made an impatient gesture. ˙His brows were raised, so that his eyes seemed larger than usual, and flashed with an angry light. ''Are you again harping on the old tune, Wolfgang? It is an offence to me. Have I not told you, again and again, that I will not sell the Word of God for money? I will not bear the shame before my friends and the world, that it should be said of me: He has preached the Gospel for filthy lucre's sake, that he might heap up riches and fare sumptuously every day. 'Freely ye have received, freely give,' saith the Lord. Did not the Man who died for me let it cost Him dearly enough? Then I too will dedicate my life to my work, neither will I accept the world's reward.''

Wolfgang, who stood upon a very friendly footing with the Doctor, here ventured to interrupt him: ''Well said, Herr Doctor; but even though for your own person you desire nothing, and despise the treasures of this earth,—yet are you not bound to provide for

those who are dependent upon you, and to secure
their future, by laying aside what will keep them from
want?"

"That I shall never do," replied Luther, with decision. "Otherwise they would put their trust not in
God, but in their possessions, and to them their hearts
would cling."

Shaking his head, Wolfgang turned, and slowly
walked across the court, soliloquizing as he went: "A
wonderful man, the Doctor, and so forth! How great
and lofty is his spirit, and how pitiable seems one of
us beside him. Such a man I never saw. He pleads
for others, that a stone would be moved to pity, but
for himself he asks nothing, although he needs it sorely. How many have, through his intercession, obtained favor from the Elector; yet he opposes those
who would report his own needs. If he accepts a
gift even from his nearest friend, it is only after
much persuasion, and for the sake of sharing it with
others. Thus he disposed of the two hundred florins
sent him recently by his grace, the Elector, and of the
hundred florins sent him by an unknown person,
through Bugenhagen. I remember with sorrow the
fine roebuck from the Elector's forest. It would have
furnished us meat for three or four days, but the Doctor must needs invite so many friends, that they quick-

ly made an end of it. I grieve for the costly flagon of glass and tin, a wedding gift from our gracious lord, which is about to follow the rest, being destined for the Pastor Agricola in Eisleben; because, forsooth, he expressed his admiration of it. I heard the Doctor whisper to his guest: "I will send it before another gets it, for my Kate would fain keep it for herself, to feast her eyes upon it.' I was secretly glad, when he could not find the flagon, in time for Agricola's birthday, for in the meantime Mistress Kate had hidden it away. But what shall it avail her? As I saw with my own eyes, the Doctor wrote to Eisleben, that for the present he was unable to keep his promise, which he greatly regretted, but he hoped soon to get the flagon into his possession.—My dear Doctor is not to be measured by the standard of ordinary mortals, and so forth. Therefore it may be regarded as a wise providence of God, that such a helpmeet was given him, who, by her housewifely virtues, her thrift, her industry, foresight and experience, can sustain her household with small means. It is the Doctor's good fortune, that his wife is of a different nature from himself, thus producing a pleasant harmony between the two, and so forth.''

The worthy Wolfgang, at the end of his soliloquy, found himself at the door of the stable, where stood his lathe, and where the Doctor, when his mind was wearied with study, often helped him at his work. He heard footsteps behind him, and turning, saw Luther coming toward him.

"Let us turn the lathe, dear Wolf," said Luther, "and test the new tools which my friend Link sent me from Nuremberg. I am ill-disposed for other work. My breast is sorely oppressed, and my breathing is difficult."

Wolfgang brought out the tools and they set to work. Before many minutes had passed, a maid-servant rushed from the house. Her face was flushed, and tears were in her eyes. "Herr Doctor!" she exclaimed, "Herr Doctor."

Luther looked up from his work. "What is it, Dorothy?" and a sudden flush rose to his face. Luther understood the gestures of the excited girl, and hurrying across the court, he soon stood by the bedside of his faithful wife, who had brought him a precious gift. He lay there, gazing upon his father with great clear eyes,—a strong, handsome boy. But an hour ago, Katharine was walking in the garden, and now God had given her her firstborn son.

In the joy of his overflowing heart, Luther took the child into his arms, looked into its eyes, and caressed it. "O thou dear, heavenly Father," he exclaimed, "how has poor brother Martin deserved so great a blessing! Behold this is pure, unmerited grace, and humbles me to the dust, so that I could weep.— My dear child, thou art most heartily welcome. My heart already beats with love toward thee, who hast yet done nothing to call it forth. Now I can understand how God's love toward us poor creatures forestalls our love. He does not wait until we come to Him and bring Him our love, but He comes to us.— My child, thy name shall be John, that, as often as I call thee, I may remember God's mercy, which this day has visited our house. For thy grandfather's sake also, thou shalt bear his name. I can see in the spirit how his dim eyes will brighten at the tidings of thy birth, and his withered lips will glorify the name of the Lord." Turning to his wife, he said : "My dear Kate, you have made me very rich, and are daily kindling a warmer love within my heart. I would gladly give my life for you, if there were need.—But now I will hasten and call a clergyman, that this poor little heathen be made a Christian."

He reached after his cloak and hat, and left the house. An hour later, at four o'clock, the child was baptized by the Chaplain, George Roerer,—Kranach, Bugenhagen, and Jonas acting as sponsors. The custom of the time demanded that a child be baptized immediately after its birth.

With the child, a new life entered into Luther's house. A child is a tie which binds even closer those who were joined together before the altar, and is a visible reminder, that these two are pledged to inseparable companionship. Although Luther had always loved and esteemed his wife, a new tenderness now seemed to warm his heart. Katharine did not fail to perceive this increase of love, and holding her child in her arms, she often whispered, with moist eyes: "Thou sweet child! thy mother owes thee hearty thanks, for thou hast brought a great blessing into the house."

A lively competition soon arose between Katharine and her cousin, "Aunt Lena," whom Luther had received into his family after her escape from the convent, both claiming the first right to the care of the child,—Kate, because she was its mother, and the older woman because of her gratitude to those who had taken pity on her helpless condition. Whosoever saw Dr. Martin playing with his little Hans, asked himself, if this were indeed the man who had shaken the world to its very foundations; whose name was on the lips of every Christian—the hero of Worms, the prophet of the Most High? The man before whom kings and princes bowed, and whom the pope, together with his bishops, feared, more than the Grand Turk himself? How could this great man become a child again, and speak in words that a child might understand? Verily, an able and learned master was he, understanding not only the tongue of the ancient Israelites, and of the Greeks and Romans, but speaking withal the language of childhood in such a fluent manner, that it was a delight to hear him. Whence did he take the time, burdened as he was with cares of weightiest import, to play with his child and to watch his growth? In letters to his friends he had much to tell of his little Hans, of his first tooth, his first steps, and his baby prattle.—Many an one who calls himself a scholar, sits buried among his books, which are to him as children, devoting to them his whole strength, his time and his heart, while in the nursery yonder the patient mother toils for and with her living children. It seems too small a matter, to descend from the heights of spiritual life to the beginnings of human development. Martin Luther was a scholar, before whose learning many an one, who thinks he has mastered much wisdom, must hide his head. But he was far more,—being a man of a universal grasp of mind ; a genius,—great in whatever position he filled ; great, even, when he descended to small things.

There has been preserved to us a letter, written by

Luther in the year 1530, from the Castle of Coburg, to his four year old son, which is a jewel of educational wisdom, and a fitting example of the great man's skill in the language of childhood.

"Grace and Peace in Christ, my dear little son ! I am well pleased to hear that thou learnest well thy lessons and prayest diligently. Continue to do so, my son, and when I come home, I will bring thee a fine "fairing." I know of a lovely, gay garden, wherein are many children, wearing golden coats, who gather from under the trees sweet apples, pears, cherries and plums. They sing, dance and are merry, and have pretty little horses, with saddles of silver and bridles of gold. I asked the master of the garden, whose were these children ? He said : These are the children who love to pray and learn their lessons, and who are good. Then said I : Dear man, I too have a little son, whose name is Hans Luther. Might not he also come into this garden, and eat of these beautiful apples and pears, ride upon these fine horses, and play with these children ? Said the man : If he willingly prays and learns, and is good, he may come into the garden, and Lippus[1] and Jost[2] with him. And when they are all together, they shall have pipes, drums, lutes, and all sorts of stringed instruments ; and they

(1.) Melanchthon's son Philip.   (2.) Jonas' son Justus.

shall dance, and shoot with little cross bows. And he showed me a smooth lawn in the garden, prepared for dancing; there hung pipes of pure gold, drums and silver cross-bows. But it was still very early, and the children had not yet dined, therefore I could not wait for the dance. I said to the man: Dear sir, I will forthwith go, and write these things to my dear son Hans, and tell him to pray diligently, learn well and be good, that he too may come into this garden. But he has an Aunt Lena, whom he must bring with him. The man said: So it shall be. Go and write him, as you have said. Therefore, my dear little son, pray and learn cheerfully, and tell Lips and Jost to do the same, that you may together come into the garden. And herewith I commit you to the dear Lord's keeping. Greet Aunt Lena, and give her a kiss from me.

"Your loving father,   MARTIN LUTHER."

Thus he wrote, when in the Castle of Coburg, strengthened he with his prayers and his counsel the hearts of his friends, who appeared at the Diet of Augsburg, before the Emperor and the assembled dignitaries of the Empire, to confess the Protestant faith, and to obtain for the Reformation the recognition of its rights.

CHAPTER XIII.

"AS DYING, AND, BEHOLD, WE LIVE."

IN the early dawn of a hot summer's day—the 6th of July, 1527—a woman hurried through the streets of Wittenberg, and knocked at the door of the town-preacher, Bugenhagen. With anxious haste she entered the study of the reverend gentleman.

"Dear Doctor, I beg of you, for Christ's sake, come with me; my dear husband is in great anguish, and I am sorely troubled. Perhaps you may be better able, than I, to comfort him."

Bugenhagen, greatly alarmed, inquired more particularly into the condition of his friend.

Mistress Katharine, still panting from her hurried walk—for the sick man was no other than Dr. Martin Luther—replied: "His head is confused, and frightful visions arise before him. He imagines that the Devil is besetting him, who seeks to put him to shame, and to destroy the work of his life. Although I have endeavored to soothe him with loving words, he seems not to hear me, and refuses food and drink. In January he suffered in a like manner, but a tea of herbs

(124)

restored him. This time my simple remedies have been without effect."

Bugenhagen listened with painful interest. "Do no not despair, dear Mistress Luther," he said; "it is not the Devil who is at work, but his sluggish blood, which rises to his head and produces these illusions. I can easily explain the cause. His body is taking its revenge for the sins committed against it, when in the convent, out of ignorance, and from mistaken piety, he undermined his health with watching, fasting and otherwise mortifying the flesh. He sits too closely over his books, denies himself the needed recreation, and tortures his brain with overmuch study and thought. The world's enmity against the truth causes him much sorrow; the miserable peasants' war has grieved his generous spirit, and the dispute with the Swiss sacramentarians is not yet ended. All these things have given him many sad hours. But with God's help, it will pass over. I will go with you, and do what I can."

They at once repaired to the convent. The servants stood about, in anxious fear, and regarded with dismay the town-preacher, who was also Luther's confessor.

Bugenhagen found the sick man reclining in a chair, his arms hanging listlessly at his side. His friendly greeting was received with a dreary smile.

"You are heartily welcome, dear Bugenhagen. I longed to see you, that I might unburden my heart, and receive absolution. Behold, whatsoever sins I have committed during my life, in thought, word and deed, rest like a weight upon my soul, and I pray God, for Christ's sake, to have mercy on a poor sinner. Dear Bugenhagen, give me God's assurance that I shall find grace with the ever-living Father of mercies."

Deeply moved, Bugenhagen gave him absolution, and then inquired into the nature of his malady.

"Dear Dr. Gommer," Luther replied, "the torments which are now besetting me remind me of St. Paul, when he was buffeted by the messengers of Satan; for such ills there seems to be no natural cause. Because I am usually of a cheerful countenance, many think that my path is strewn with roses; but God knows how it is with me."

Bugenhagen repeated the arguments, with which he had sought to reassure Mistress Kate, but they made little impression on the sick man.

Bugenhagen then reminded Luther of the invitation they had both received, to breakfast with the Elector's marshal, Hans Löser. "The society of these men, and the fresh air will do you good. I pray you, Martin, rouse yourself." Katharine's eloquence was added to that of Bugenhagen, and finally Luther yielded to their united persuasions.

At the inn, where the breakfast was served, a chosen company was assembled. Luther ate little, but forced himself to join in the conversation. At noon he left quietly, and went to his friend Justus Jonas, the provost of All Saints' School. He sat for two hours, pouring out his heart to his friend, for Jonas was a man of wise counsel and loving sympathy. Before leaving, Luther invited his friend to visit him in the evening. When Jonas arrived at the appointed time, he found the Doctor lying on his bed, complaining of great weakness, and a constant rushing and singing in his left ear. Feeling a sudden faintness, Luther called for water, which Jonas brought and dashed into his face, This seemed to revive the sufferer. He lay back among the pillows, with wide open eyes. But suddenly his face changed ; his body grew cold, and shook as in an ague fit. With difficulty he folded his hands, and a fervent prayer rose from his lips :

" My God, if thou hast ordained this to be my last hour, I submit myself to Thy Will. O Lord, rebuke me not in thine anger, neither chasten me in thy hot displeasure. Have mercy upon me, O Lord ;

for I am weak : O Lord, heal me ; for my bones are vexed. My soul is also sore vexed : But Thou, O Lord, how long ? Return, O Lord, deliver my soul : Oh save me, for Thy mercy's sake. For in death there is no remembrance of Thee : in the grave who shall give thee thanks ? I am weary with my groaning ; all the night make I my bed to swim ; I water my couch with my tears. Mine eye is consumed because of grief; it waxeth old, because of all mine enemies. Depart from me, all ye workers of iniquity, for the Lord hath heard the voice of my weeping. The Lord hath heard my supplication ; the Lord will receive my prayer. Let all mine enemies be ashamed and sore vexed : let them return and be ashamed suddenly. Lord, Thou hast been our dwelling place in all generations. Amen."

While he was praying, Katharine had entered the room, bringing with her Augustin Schurf, the family physician, who at once ordered the patient to be wrapped in heated cloths. Luther seemed to observe nothing of what was passing. His thoughts were with God, and his eyes were turned heavenward. Again he prayed, and all folded their hands in tearful reverence :

" O death, where is thy sting ? O grave, where is thy victory ? Thanks be to God, which giveth us the victory through our Lord Jesus Christ. I lay me down in peace and sleep; for Thou, Lord, only makest me dwell in safety. Lord Jesus Christ receive my spirit. I take refuge in Thy wounds; Thy righteousness upholds me,—Thou art our only Mediator and High Priest, who bearest the sins of the world. Dear Lord, Thou hast not counted Thy servant worthy, after the manner of the blessed martyrs, to shed his blood for Thee; yet will I take comfort in the example of St. John, to whom also this boon was denied, albeit he wrote a book against the Antichrist, far more effective than any book of mine!"

Turning to his friends, he continued: "Dear, faithful friends; lest after my death the world should say I had recanted, I ask you to witness this my confession. I declare, with a clear conscience, that I have taught none but the true and wholesome doctrine, concerning faith, love, the cross, the sacraments, and other articles of the Christian religion, according to God's Word and at His command, Who alone has guided me in this matter, and has drawn and urged me forward, without any will of mine. I testify to those who have reproached me with too great sharpness against the papists and fanatics, that I have experienced no remorse in the matter, having never sought any man's hurt, but rather the conversion and salva-

9

tion of my enemies.   I would fain abide a little longer, inasmuch as many a word still remains to be said
against the fanatics and the Sacramentarians.   But
God's Will be done.   Christ is stronger than Belial,
and can raise up servants out of stones, who will fight
in His Name."

His eyes then sought his wife, who stood apart from
the others, weeping bitterly.   He beckoned her to
come nearer, took her hand and said : "Dearest Kate,
I pray you, if the dear Lord take me from hence, that
you submit to His gracious Will.   You are my true
and lawful wife.   Of that you shall have no doubt,—
let the blind world say what it will.   Be guided by
the Word of God ; cling to that, and you will have a
never-failing support against the Devil and all evil
tongues."

He lay back ; his breath came hard, like that of a
dying man.   Then he turned and asked : "Where is
my dear little son Hans ?"

The child was brought, and greeted his sick father
with a smile.   Tenderly the cold hand caressed his
warm, rosy cheeks, and the pallid lips pronounced a
father's blessing : "O thou poor child !   I commit
my dear wife and my fatherless child into the hands
of my loving, faithful God.   You have nothing, for I
leave you no earthly goods ; but God has enough for all.

Dear Lord, I thank Thee from my heart, that it hath pleased Thee to make me poor in worldly things ; I can therefor leave to my wife and child neither house nor land, neither money nor goods. As Thou gavest me them, so I return them to Thee. Thou rich and faithful God, do Thou sustain, teach, and provide for them, even as thou didst sustain, teach and provide for me, O Thou Father of the fatherless, Thou Friend of the widow."

Katharine's heart was wruug with grief.° God, in his unsearchable wisdom, was laying a heavy sorrow upon her. For two years she had enjoyed the blessedness of her union with this man ; henceforth she and her child must stand alone, poor and defenceless ; dependent upon the uncertain favor of human friendship ; exposed to the scorn and hatred of enemies, who would make the living feel the insults they might no longer heap upon the dead !—When she thought of herself and the child, her heart seemed well-nigh breaking ; but when she looked at her husband, and heard his prayer in her behalf, strength was given her, to endure in silence, and even to speak words of comfort to the sufferer. Bending over him, she said gently: "My dearest Doctor, if it be God's Will, I would rather you were with Him, than with me. I grieve not for myself and for my child only, but for the many good Christian people, who still have need of you. Do not, my dearest husband, trouble yourself about me.   I commend you to God's holy Will, and hope and trust that He will graciously spare you."

It seemed as though her words inspired the others with renewed courage.   The physician, who had given up all hope, ordered the cold limbs to be again warmed and rubbed.   Love and friendship labored faithfully to restore the precious life, and prayer after prayer rose to heaven.

Then came the merciful answer: "Behold, he shall not die, but live!"   It seemed like a miracle when the color returned to the pallid face, and the drops of moisture which appeared on the sick man's forehead seemed like dew from Heaven.

The physician exclaimed: "He lives! He lives!" As one intoxicated by the sudden change from despair to hope, the loving wife fell at the feet of him to whom God had revealed the means of preserving her husband's life.

.   .   .   .

His life was out of danger, but his soul—as he said —was still tossed to and fro between Christ and Belial, and miserably bruised.   He supposed that he would all his life long be compelled to wade through deep waters of tribulation, but would gladly submit, if it contributed to the glory of his God and Saviour.

Then God sent him an angel of consolation, which to others was an angel of terror. That which cast them down, raised up Dr. Martin. That which shook the faith of strong men, and drove them to despair, restored to him the vigor of his faith and his heroic trust in the living God.

He that sits upon the pale horse rode in at the gates of Wittenberg, holding in his hand the naked sword, to which all living things must succumb. It was that terror of terrors—the plague.

The citizens were panic-stricken, and a stubborn fatalism seemed to seize upon their minds. The Elector's command came from Torgau to the University: "Let teachers and students leave Wittenberg, and seek safety in Jena!" In the Augustinian Convent sat the foremost among the teachers of the University, and in holy defiance replied to the Elector's anxious demand: "I shall remain; I dare not go!" Another urgent request came to him from his sovereign, but his answer was the same: "I shall remain; I dare not go."

Fear, that most effective ally of the plague, had taken possession of the people. But Luther was unacquainted with fear. In his ears rang the Saviour's words: "The good shepherd giveth his life for his sheep. But he that is an hireling seeth the wolf coming, and leaveth the sheep, and fleeth." With Bugenhagen and Roerer, who had also remained, he visited the plague-stricken houses, bringing help to the living and consolation to the dying. Many died in his arms, breathing pestilence into his face,—but he seemed steeled against contagion, guarded by his fidelity to his people and by his trust in God. And behold, the more lavishly the strength of his body was consumed in this loving service, the more abundantly streamed into his soul a new, God-given vigor. The shadows of melancholy vanished, the Devil's hold was loosed,—and clear in the heaven of his inner world shone his spiritual sun, Jesus Christ.

God enabled him, in many instances, to wrest from death its prey. With all the might of his influence he combated the false fears of the people, and directed them to seek help from God. He reassured the timid, and revived their sinking faith. He rebuked the foolhardy, who tempted God by refusing the necessary remedies. He battled with the superstitious notion that persons were cured by transmitting the disease to others, and thundered in holy indignation against such as in fiendish malice, forced their way into houses as yet uninfected.

Of his own danger he took no thought ; nor that his precious life must be preserved to the Church. All his life long he had left the disposal of his affairs with God ; with the same calm trustfulness he placed his life in the Father's hands, and his countenance wore the same peaceful serenity in the chambers of the dying, as it had formerly worn in the pulpit or lecture hall.

Not content with assuming the duties of pastor and physician among the sick, he wrote the Protestants in Halle a letter of condolence upon the death of Winkler, a preacher of the Gospel, who had been assassinated by the Romanists. He worked at his exposition of the prophet Zechariah, and made the necessary preparations for the approaching parish-visitation.

Thus he remained at his post, in unshaken fidelity, —as a good shepherd of the flock committed to his care. Silent and ashamed, his enemies beheld him enforcing his doctrine with his life.

Beside him, full of heroic courage, stood the wife whom God had given him. Ministering with the tenderest devotion to his wants, she assisted him in his labors among the sick, and with ready kindness opened her doors to all who came to her for help. The physician Schurf, with his family, had taken refuge in Luther's house. His wife fell ill, and plague spots appeared on her body. Margaret von Mochau, another member of Luther's household, fell sick. Unmindful of herself, Katharine nursed the sufferers, receiving strength from on high for the fulfilling of her Samaritan's work.

Then came news of the death of a dear friend, the young wife of the Chaplain Roerer, who, with her new-born child, fell a prey to the plague. Katharine's heart failed her at this fresh blow. Even Luther began to despair, and the storm of new trials threatened to overthrow the strong man. Bugenhagen, who, with his family, had moved into Luther's house, sought in vain to comfort his friend. Luther saw his wife growing daily weaker, and his little son Hans was beginning to droop.

But behold, God knew better than men, how to raise up the sinking hearts. On the 10th of December, Dr. Martin stood by the bedside of his beloved wife, giving thanks for the mother's life, and for the new life that had entered their house. Holding a new-born child in his arms, he bent down to little Hans and said: "See, Hans, God has given you a little sister!"

The Winter's storms scattered the last germs of the pestilence. The survivors breathed freely, and gave thanks for their deliverance, and by April the fugitives returned. Luther and his wife prayed:

"Thou art the God that doest wonders; Thou hast made known thy power and goodness towards us. In many a household, the members have been made less, but in ours there is one more."

Luther wrote to his friend, Justus Jonas: "The dear Lord has given me a daughter, my sweet, little Elizabeth, and has relieved me of all anxiety concerning my wife. The pestilence entered our house, but the Lord spared us. The plague took our pigs instead, of which five have fallen. I am happy, and thank the Lord, that the angel of death was content with such inferior prey. The plague is now dead and buried."

The returning friends flocked to his house, to convince themselves that the man of God still lived. They had left him bowed down and oppressed with care. They found him cured and, inspired with new strength, as with glowing eyes he welcomed them: "As dying, and, behold, we live."

CHAPTER XIV.

BEREAVED, AND COMFORTED.

AT a short distance from Wittenberg, near the E'lster gate, a well is shown to this day, called Luther's Well, it having been discovered and opened by Luthther in the year 1520. The miner's son had a sure instinct for all minerals and treasures hidden in the earth.

Near this well, among the trees, and within hearing of the rushing waters of the Elbe, Luther in the year 1526 built himself a summer-house, which Katharine's skillful hand beautified and furnished most conveniently. It was a pleasant spot and Mistress Luther was rewarded for her pains by frequent visits from her friends. In this peaceful retreat Luther loved to gather around him his friends, Melanchthon, Cruciger and Auerhahr, and with them work at the translation of the New Testament. Here the fourth chapter according to St. John, telling of Jacob's Well, was completed.

It was a warm, sunny May-day in the year 1528. The Spring sunshine had caused the tender leaves to

burst their buds; the garden flowers vied with the
wild flowers in furnishing sweet food to the bees and
butterfliés; even the farmers' plough horses neighed
with delight.

In the summer house near the Elster-gate, sat Dr.
Martin with his lute. The Spring-time had seized
upon his heart, for when all nature is singing for joy,
Dr. Martin cannot keep silence. Beside him sat Mistress Katharine, with her baby in her arms, lost in
happy dreams,—now listening to the notes of the
lute, now resting her eyes upon the lovely landscape.
When the Doctor, changing from his free, fresh im-
provisation, played the air which he had com-
posed especially for his little son Hans, Katharine
hummed the tune, while Hans, who was playing on
the floor with a wooden horse, looked up attentively,
for he knew well that it was his song.

The child was now two years old, a blooming, vigorous boy, and already sufficiently master of his mother tongue, to make his wants known. The wooden
horse, a product of Wolfgang's lathe, was his favorite
toy, his childish imagination investing it with all the
qualities of the living animal. It was lodged in a
stall, built in a corner of the room, was each night
provided with hay and straw, and in times of sickness
neither medicine nor care were wanting.

With heartfelt pleasure the parents' eyes rested upon their first-born, and Katharine said to her husband: "If God gives grace, Hans will be the joy and comfort of our old age." Glancing at the child in her arms, she continued, with a troubled face:—"But when I look at our sweet little Elizabeth, I am mindful of the Apostle's admonition,—to have as though we had not. She is the child of my fears, born amid fears, and nurtured in fear to this present time. See, how pale is the little face, and how deep the shadows under her eyes.

Luther leaned over and stroked the little hand: "Dear wife, the Apostle's word applies not only to a feeble child,—we should possess all our children, as though we possessed them not. The Lord has but lent them to us, and claims them again, when it pleases Him."

A look of deep sorrow clouded Katharine's face: "Doubtless you are right, dearest Doctor; yet it is better to see them come than go, and if we were forced to yield up one of them, I believe my heart would break. Ah my little Elizabeth, my darling child—" She pressed her lips to her pale, little face, and hot tears gushed from her eyes. The Doctor felt his own growing moist, and was glad to see his friends, Melanchthon, with Master Reichenbach and his wife, coming towards their house.

"We thought," cried Mistress Elsa, "that we must seek you here, as we failed to find you at home. How lovely is this Spring day." ·

Frau Elsa sat down beside Katharine, and the men with Dr. Martin.

"You have a fine scent, my friends," he began, "that has betrayed to you, what his grace the Elector, has sent me. I, for my part, can boast of a true prophetic instinct, which told me that some of my friends would seek me out to-day. Therefore I have caused the gift to be brought out here." He pointed to a corner, where lay a small cask ; beside it stood a large earthen jug. "It is said to be choice Spanish wine, for Dr. Martin's refreshment."

"He is a kindly gentleman, our Elector," returned Reichenbach. "But you, dear Doctor, must follow his advice, and yourself drink the wine, that was sent for your refreshment."

Luther was already filling the jug from the cask. "What would you have, dear Reichenbach ? Would the wine refresh me, if I drank it alone? Just as divided joy is double joy, so, to me, divided wine is double wine."

He brought the jug to the syndic. When the latter still refused, Melanchthon said, with a significant glance : "Take it, Reichenbach ; the Doctor is now

forty-five years old.   We cannot change his nature in
these matters.''

The wine was passed around, and in the intercourse
with his beloved friends, Luther's inborn happy humor burst forth with irresistible charm, as though he
had never in his life been sad or heavy-hearted.   Towards evening other citizens of Wittenberg came out
to enjoy the balmy air.   Luther made them all welcome.   They talked together of many things,—of the
affairs of the city of Wittenberg, and of those of the
kingdom of God, until it grew late, and Wolfgang
came limping out from town, with warm wraps for
Mistress Luther and the children, and well-meant advice to the Doctor, not to linger in the night-air.
Luther readily yielded, and all returned to town together.

The roses in Luther's garden were blooming gloriously, delighting not only the Doctor, but all those
whom he invited into his garden, to view the wonderful works of God, and those into whose houses he sent
generous nosegays of the fragrant flowers.   But greater was his joy, when he saw the roses slowly appearing
in little Elizabeth's cheeks.   The physician, Augustin
Schurf, smiled sadly when he saw the father's fond delusion,—he knew that under the roses death was at
work.   Soon the little face grew pale again, and with

hearts doubly saddened by disappointed hope, the parents stood beside their dying child, and tasted the bitterness of death. They prayed for its life, but God said : "Give me the child."

As the last struggle was drawing near, Luther, with a supreme effort of renunciation, exclaimed : "Lord, Thy will be done !" Katharine cried aloud : "O dear Father, let this cup pass from us. It is so bitter, methinks I cannot drink it."

When Luther saw his wife's grief, tears burst from the strong man's eyes and he wept like a child. This roused Katharine from her sorrow, and seeing her husband's pain, she strove to comfort him. And Luther, having received, was again able to give. He walked behind the little coffin, as it was carried to the grave, accompanied by weeping friends, and there spoke words of comfort to all present. Here he again experienced, more fully than ever, how great a treasure is the precious Word of God, which is most powerful and life-giving, when the soul is passing through darkness and sorrow.

Wolfgang made a little cross of wood, which he set upon the grave, and Luther wrote upon it : *"Hic dormit Elisabeth, filiola Martini Lutheri, Anno 1528 "* "Here sleeps Elizabeth, Martin Luther's little daughter."

. . . .

It was long, before Katharine's loving heart could
cast aside its sorrow.   Yet she was made acquainted
with one of the blessings of affliction, namely, the
hearty sympathy and affection of the members of her
household.   Her servants, as well as the boarders,
were eager to serve her, as though each one, as far as
in him lay, desired to comfort the bereaved mother,
and Katharine was deeply grateful for their loving
service.

Better than they, the Lord supplied her loss. When
the lilies of the valley bloomed on little Elizabeth's
grave, the happy mother's thanksgiving rose heavenward: "The Lord hath taken away, the Lord hath
given.   Blessed be the name of the Lord."   In his
study Luther sat and wrote in great haste :

"Grace and Peace in Christ, my dear Amsdorf!
The gracious God has regarded our sorrow, and has
sent us in place of our little dead maiden, a living
one.   I pray you, therefore, make haste, that it may
not longer remain a heathen, but speedily, by means
of the blessed Sacrament, be enrolled in Heaven as an
heir of eternal life."

When the sacred act had been performed, Luther
took his daughter upon his arm and said : "My dear
little Lena, thou art doubly welcome,—for thine own
sake, and for the sake of thy departed sister, who

lives again in thee ; for when I look at thee, me-thinks I again behold my little Elizabeth.''

Then, turning to his wife, he bent down over the pale face, and said : "You dearest wife, how can I thank you for this precious gift ! What were Dr. Martin, without his Kate ! Since I have you, I am no longer poor, but a rich man indeed ! If Thou lovest me, O Lord my God, do Thou preserve and bless this dear life.''

10

CHAPTER XV.

ALONE.

KATHARINE sat alone in her husband's study,—that famous spot, whence Luther directed his attacks upon the Papacy. For five long months the Doctor had been absent at the Castle of Coburg. There, by the Elector's desire, he remained during the continuance of the Diet of Augsburg, where he was unable to be present, by reason of the Imperial interdict. Yet he was near enough to aid the Protestants with his counsel, and infuse into their hearts some of his own spiritual strength.

Although the reformer was often called from home by his many duties, Katharine could never accustom herself to his absence. Her life seemed bereft of its dignity and its chief delight, when she could neither see her husband's face, nor hear his voice. She lived for him only, nay more,—all that gave purpose to her existence, and made her life worth living, came from him. As she rested under the shadow of this great man, life unfolded to her its fullness. She had no desire to glory before the world, as the wife of the great-

(146)

est and the most renowned man of his time. To be overshadowed by his greatness, to receive from the abundance of his spiritual riches, seemed to her a great and an enviable privilege. To forget herself, to serve him in humble love, was her most cherished duty.

Her husband has therefore sung her praises in every key: "I have truly a faithful and God-fearing wife, in whom the heart of her husband may safely trust, as Solomon saith. She is willing and obedient in all things, more than I dared hope for. I could not find a more obedient wife, were I to hew one out of stone. Therefore I love my Kate far better than myself, and I would rather die, than that harm should come to her and the little ones. I esteem her more highly than the kingdom of France and the principality of Venice. For this is God's highest gift and grace,—a virtuous, loving, diligent, God-fearing wife, with whom thou canst live in peace, and to whom thou mayest safely entrust all that thou hast."

Luther had left for her assistance and protection the brothers Peter and Jerome Weller; but they, together with all the numerous household, could not fill the void caused by his absence. There was but one Luther, as there is but one sun in the heavens. When the sun goes down, the moon and all the myriad stars cannot take its place.

Katharine was mending little Hans' jacket, but her thoughts were not with her needle. She soon put her work aside, and unlocking a chest, brought out a pocket of yellow leather, in which she preserved the letters received from Augsburg and Coburg. Although she knew their contents by heart, she read them again. Deep, calm joy brightened her face, as the evening sunshine brightens the summer fields; for in these letters she had new and visible testimony, that Dr. Martin loved his wife with a full, true love, and that the respect of other good men was not wanting.

She smiled, as she unfolded the first letter, written in a merry, jesting vein, each word expressing delight in his lofty abode, "in the kingdom of the birds."

"Grace and Peace in Christ! My dear Kate! We have safely reached our Sinai; but we purpose to make a Tabor of it, and build three tabernacles, one for the Psalter, one for the Prophets, and one for Æsop.[1] First of all, your old lover wishes to announce to you that Dr. Martin has become a king, or at least a prince, and dwells in a high castle, with thirty serving

---

(1) It was Luther's intention to translate the fables of Æsop, to "adapt them for youth and common men, that they should be of some use to the Germans." There are thirteen fables of his version, rendered in the simplest popular language.

men, in gay coats, together with twelve watchmen,
and two trumpeters in the tower. It is a very quiet
place, and favorable to study, except that a great tumult is constantly going on in the air without. Under our windows there is a little wood, where the ra-
vens and jackdaws are holding a diet. There is a continual coming and going, and such chattering, day
and night, that one might think they were all drunken
with wine. Young and old are cawing and croaking
together, that I marvel that their ears and throats can
endure it. I should like to know, if any of this nobility
still remain with you, for methinks they are gathered
here from all quarters of the earth. I have not yet
seen their Emperor, but the nobles and great ones
among them are always before our eyes—not in costly
raiment, but all alike arrayed in black, and all alike
grey-eyed. They also sing but one tune, with the various voices of young and old, great and small. They
care not for stately palaces and halls; their hall is arched with the fair, wide heavens; their floor is the
earth, tricked out with green boughs; and their walls
are as wide as the ends of the earth. They ask not
for horses and soldiers, for they have feathery pinions,
upon which they fly from the anger of men. Great
and mighty lords are they; but what decisions they
have arrived at, I have not yet heard; although as far

as I could learn through an interpreter, they are plan-
ning a mighty crusade against the fields of wheat, barley, oats and other grains, where many an one will per-
form deeds of valor, and win his spurs by his prowess.
Thus we are here present at this diet, hearing and seeing with much pleasure and goodwill, how the princes,
lords, and other estates of the empire sing so merrily
and fare so well.   With especial pleasure we see them
strut about, wipe their bills and hasten to the attack
upon the grain-fields.   We wish them good luck, and
that one and all they may be spitted on a hedge stake.
Methinks they are no other than the papists and soph-
ists, with their clamoring and writing, who are here
assembled before me, to show me what useful folk they
are, devouring what is upon the earth, and chattering
for pastime.

"To-day we heard the first nightingale; she mis-
trusted the month of April.   The weather has been
fair and lovely; and we have had no rain, save only
yesterday a little.   Perhaps it has been otherwise with
you.   Look well to the house, and God be with you.

"MARTIN LUTHER.

"*April the 28th, 1530.*"

Katharine folded the letter carefully, and took up
another, in a different handwriting.

"It pleases me much," she said softly to herself,

" that his friends remember me so kindly." Then she read the letter, which Melanchthon had written her, shortly after his arrival in Augsburg :

" God's grace and blessing ! Honorable, virtuous Mistress Luther : This is to inform you that we have safely reached Augsburg, for which God be praised !— and have left the Doctor at Coburg, as he has doubtless written you. But I hope soon to be with him. I pray you, write me how it goes with you, and how the captain has behaved with regard to the grain. If I can serve you in anything, I will do it with all diligence. The chancellors, Dr. Gregory Brück and Dr. Christian Baier, who will read before the Diet the Protestant confession of faith, send you greetings and good wishes. God keep you.

" PHILIPP MELANCHTHON.

" Augsburg, Wednesday after St. Walpurgis."

Underneath was written : " Dear friend, I too wish you, and Hans, little Lena and Aunt Lena much pleasure. Kiss my dearest boy in my name.

" JUSTUS JONAS."

On the outer edge was scribbled : " I too, John Agricola, of Eisleben, wish you well, dear Mistress Luther."

Two tears fell upon the letter, which, like the others, showed signs of much handling.

" How God turns evil into good," thought Kate.
" The parting from my husband was a sore trial, yet
as its sweet fruits I have these precious letters, whence I
perceive that I am well loved, and faithfully remembered."

Another followed, also in a strange handwriting.
Veit Dietrich, a member of her family, who, with
Luther's nephew, Cyriac Kaufman, had accompanied
the Doctor, answered a letter which Katharine, soon
after Lena's birthday, had sent with a portrait of the
child, to Coburg.

" God's greeting, dear Mistress Luther ! You have
done a good work in sending the picture to the Reverend Doctor, for it drives away many heavy thoughts.
He has fastened it to the wall, opposite our table.
When he first saw it, he failed to recognize little Lena.
' Why,' he said, ' have they made my Lena so dark ? '
But now it pleases him well, and seems to him more
and more like Lena's face. She resembles Hans
greatly, especially about the nose, and mouth, and
eyes. Dear Mistress Luther, I pray you, have no anxiety about the Doctor. He is again, thank God, well
and of good cheer. He has suffered much, not only
from the Augsburg troubles, and from bodily pain,—
but from grief at the death of his father. For a whole

day he withdrew from us into his room, taking only
his Psalter with him, and weeping bitterly. But all
this he has borne and overcome, as a true hero. Dear
Mistress Luther, I cannot sufficiently extol his stead-
fastness and serenity, his faith and hopefulness,
during these troublous times. But he constantly
nourishes these virtues with diligent study of the divine Word. He passes at least three hours, the best
hours of the day, in prayer. Once it was my good
fortune to hear him pray. Great God, how strong a
faith breathed from his words. He prays to God with
such deep reverence, with such power and confidence,
as though he were speaking to his father or to a friend.
'I know,' he said, 'that Thou art our God and Father; therefore I am assured that Thou wilt put them to
shame, that persecute Thy children. The danger is
Thine, as well as ours. Thine is the cause; we have
put our hands to it, because we needs must. Therefore defend Thou it, and give it the victory.' It was
thus that I, standing afar off, heard him pray, with a
loud, clear voice. My heart burned within me, when
he spoke with God in so confident, reverent and child
like a manner, insisting upon God's promises, given
in the Psalms,—as one who is certain of obtaining all
that he asks.—Behold, dear Mistress Luther, this great
man is your husband; for which you have cause to

praise God.—How fares my Hans, and my dear little
Lena? Kiss them for me. Yourself and Aunt Lena I commend to God, and together with the Doctor
and your Cousin Cyriac, send you greetings.

"VEIT DIETRICH."

Katharine searched further, and brought out two
more letters, in her husband's strong, rugged handwriting.

"Grace and Peace in Christ! My dear Kate,—
The messenger is in haste, and I can write you but a
few words. Tell Dr. Pommer and the rest, that I will
soon write more. We have had no tidings from Augsburg, but are waiting hourly for letters. It is rumored
that the reply of our opponents will be read publicly;
but that those of our party have been refused a copy
of the refutation. I know not, if it be true. Where
matters are thus kept in the dark, our friends will not
long remain.

"Since St. Laurence's day I have been very well,
and have felt no ringing in my head. Therefore I am
inclined to study, for heretofore the ringing has greatly tormented me. Greetings to all. More the next
time. God be with you. Amen. Pray diligently,—
it is of need, and God will help us.

"MARTIN LUTHER.

" August the 14th, 1530."

To this letter Katharine had sewed another, which reached her at the same time:

"Grace and Peace in Christ, my dear Kate! After I had sealed my letter, dispatches were brought me from Augsburg, and I detained the messenger that he might carry them also to you. From them you will learn how matters stand at Augsburg,—almost as I wrote you. Let Peter Wellér read them for you, or Dr. Pommer. May God help further, as He has begun. Amen. I cannot write more. The messenger is impatient to go. Greet all the dear ones, especially Hans Luther and his schoolmaster, to whom I will write soon. Greet Aunt Lena and all the others. We are eating ripe grapes, although this has been a wet month. God be with you all.

"MARTIN LUTHER.

"*From the Wilderness, on the Day of the Assumption of the V. Mary.*"

Then followed what was best of all, wrapped in rose colored paper—Luther's letter to his little son. Katharine's eyes grew moist as she read the precious words, and from her heart rose a prayer in behalf of the great, the glorious Dr. Martin Luther.

CHAPTER XVI.

GOD'S INN.

WHILE Katharine was refolding the letters and tying them with a scarlet ribbon, her niece Elsa Kaufman[1] came into the room, and announced that a stranger, who gave his name as Urbanus Rhegius, desired to speak with Mistress Luther, having come directly from Coburg.

Katharine hurried into the court. There, under the great pear-tree, the Doctor's favorite resting place, sat a distinguished looking man, who at her approach, rose, and with great politeness advanced to meet her.

"God's greeting to you, dear Mistress Luther," he began, his foreign accent reminding her somewhat of the dialect spoken by Baumgaertner. "I regard it as a special piece of good fortune, to become acquainted with the wife of the great man, whom I met lately for the first time; and to be permitted to bring you his greetings, as I am passing through Wittenberg."

(1) She was the orphan daughter of Luther's sister, whom, with her brother Cyriac and her sister Lena, Luther had taken into his family.

(156)

"How fares my dear lord?" asked Katharine, a blush of pleased anticipation mantling her cheeks.

"He is well and of good courage. In his great goodness and condescension he gave me a whole day of his precious time. And truly, I never experienced a happier day; for Dr. Luther is a powerful theologian. I always esteemed him greatly, but now I hold him higher than ever before, having myself seen and heard what neither pen nor words can describe. His books betoken his great mind, but when one hears him speak, with the spirit of an Apostle, on divine matters, he must needs confess: Luther is too great for wiseacres to pass judgment upon him. He is, and remains the greatest theologian in the world."

In her happy confusion, Katharine found no words to answer him. As his eyes wandered over the place, he said: "Here, then, is the spot where he dwells,— 'God's Inn,' where all that are persecuted for the Gospel's sake, find shelter. Tell me, dear Mistress Luther, how can you, with your small means, feed and clothe so many? I scarcely believed my ears, when the Reverend Doctor told me, that his entire income was two hundred florins."

With a smile, Katharine pointed to the stables and barn-yard. "Do you hear those sounds, dear sir? When the larder is empty, the stable and the garden must replenish it. Yet even this would not suffice, were it not for the generous kindness of good people. Especially is the hand of our gracious Elector ever open toward us. But the Doctor is of a peculiar nature; he refuses all help,—fearing that God would reward him with temporal goods, while he strives only for heavenly treasures. Knowing my husband to be thus reluctant, they bring their gifts to me, and I do not hesitate to receive with ·pleasure and gratitude what is offered in love, and is sorely needed for our poor. For although I am careful, I have not been able to prevent the Doctor from incurring some debts, through aiding his friends."

Rhegius listened with eager attention, and pointing to the large side wing, he asked : "And is your whole house full, Mistress Luther?"

"Yes. A long row of boarders sit at my table. A few are able to pay me for what they receive, but the larger number have nothing else to give, than a "thank you." And I am well content, for thus far we have not suffered want, and I would rather serve them all without a reward, if it were possible."

"Are you going to build, Mistress Luther? I see in yonder corner a pile of bricks and tiles."

"Our house is large and roomy enough, dear sir, but old and ruinous. The Doctor consented to ac-

cept the building material, which the Town Council
sent him in recognition of his services during the time
of the plague.''

With growing surprise and pleasure the stranger's
eyes rested upon Mistress Katharine, who, changing
the conversation, said to him: "Your speech has a
foreign sound, dear sir. Where is your home, if I
may ask?''

"I am a Suabian by birth," returned Rhegius, "and
a theologian by profession,—but only a small one, not
worthy to unloose the latchet of Dr. Martin's shoes,—
yet desirous of laboring with all my strength in the
vineyard of the Lord.''

"Please be seated, dear Master Rhegius," urged
Katharine, "I will call some of our young men, that
they may hear your report of the Doctor; and I will
prepare you some refreshment.''

Katharine hurried across the court and entered the
wing, whence she soon returned with the brothers
Peter and Jerome Weller, little Hans' schoolmasters.
While they joined the stranger, plying him with many
eager questions, Katharine brought a bottle of home-
brewed beer from the cellar, and went to the kitchen,
to prepare the traveller's repast.

Before she had finished, Elsa announced a new arrival. "Dear Mistress Luther, a woman stands with-

out.   She has the look of a queen, and yet one could
weep to see her sorrowful face.   She asked me if the
doctor had returned, and seemed much distressed
when I told her he was still absent.   Then she questioned me, whether Mistress Luther had a merciful
heart, and begged to see you."

Katharine felt uneasy.   Charging Elsa with the
stranger's meal, she went to the great hall.   Pausing
at the door, she saw before her a woman of a tall, majestic figure, whose appearance affected her strangely.
An expression of blended dignity and gentleness rested upon her face, veiled with a look of unspeakable sadness.   As if in expectation of a greeting or a
question, her soft, pleading eyes sought Katharine's
face, until, like Elsa, she felt her own filling with
tears.

" Who are you, dear lady ?" asked Katharine, holding out her hand in welcome.

The stranger answered wearily : " My husband sits
upon a throne, and wears an Elector's crown ; but I
have not where to lay my head."

Katharine started : " Merciful God ! You are the
unhappy wife of the Elector of Brandenburg ! "

" Does my presence alarm you?" she asked, with
the suspicious sensitiveness peculiar to the unfortunate.
" Then I will go,—although it is with a heavy heart I

relinquish the hope of finding peace under the great reformer's roof. For the Gospel's sake my lord's anger pursues me; and because I venerate Dr. Martin's doctrine as being the Word of God, the Elector has threatened to immure me."

Katharine's heart beat high, and she would have folded the unfortunate woman in her arms, but the inborn reverence for the wife of a crowned head restrained her. She grasped the hand of the princess, saying warmly: "This house is open to all who are weary and heavy laden, but especially to those who suffer for the Gospel's sake."

A gleam of joy brightened the unhappy woman's face, and with difficulty restraining her tears, she answered: "May He bless you for those words, who said: 'Inasmuch as ye have done it unto one of the least of these my brethren, ye have done it unto me.' "

Katharine, after taking a hasty leave of Master Rhegius, led her guest to a quiet room, overlooking the garden. The noble lady's gracious bearing soon overcame Katharine's timidity, and they conversed together as old friends.

Katharine then learned the truth of the story which rumor had spread abroad, and mingled with many falsehoods. The Electress had incurred the anger of

11

her papist husband by her adherence to the evangelical faith, and especially by a secret celebration of the Lord's Supper in both kinds, which was betrayed to him, and roused in him a fury of passion.   He swore in his anger, that neither sun nor moon should again shine upon the heretic.   To save her husband from committing a crime, she fled to Torgau, seeking refuge with the Elector of Saxony.   He assigned to her the castle of Lichtenburg on the Elbe, and she accepted his kindness with gratitude.   But in time the isolation and the lack of all spiritual nourishment caused her inner life to wither and pine.   She had therefore come secretly to Wittenberg, to be near the fountain of living water, where her soul might find strength and repose.

Katharine expressed her regret at her husband's absence, and begged the Electress to content herself in her company, until the Doctor's return. .

Deeply moved, the princess fell upon Katharine's neck, and this silent embrace was the beginning of a warm and lasting friendship.   Two hearts were brought near to each other, which, however different their outward circumstances, yet were one in their aspirations after the one thing needful.   Katharine soon discovered that fame had not exaggerated the gentleness, nobility and piety of the Electress of Brandenburg;

while the latter found herself irresistibly attracted by the strong, upright, loving nature, by the childlike simplicity and tender heart of Mistress Luther. With unconcealed pleasure she watched Katharine, as with energetic discipline, with a clear eye and a firm hand she guided and ruled her extensive establishment. She was fond of helping here and there, and especially glad to occupy herself with the children. Good Aunt Lena stepped into the background without a murmur, and felt no pang of jealousy, when the thankless Hans in his admiration of the new " Aunt Elizabeth " could at times forget all the love and care that had been lavished upon him.

Katharine's feeling of loneliness was banished. As she devoted her spare moments to the sorely tried woman, she felt as though a higher duty were ennobling the common-place routine of her daily life ; and her contentment grew, as she perceived that the patient sufferer found in her house the rest she sought, and was able to look forward to the dawning of a brighter day.

Then a letter arrived from Luther to his " dear Kate," announcing his return, and promising to bring to his son Hans a fine, large book of pure sugar, which Cousin Cyriac had brought from the garden, of which he had written.

CHAPTER XVII.

PEACE.

IT was a still, sultry morning in August, 1532. Heavy clouds covered the sky and tempered somewhat the heat of the sun. Fido, the little dog, stretched himself lazily upon his bed, and the pigeons on the house-top hung their wings. In the court-yard of Luther's house, however, there was bustling activity, as if in preparation for some festivity. Wolfgang was helping his mistress fill the clear, home-brewed ale into jugs, when the trumpeter from the tower of the town-church proclaimed the sixth hour. Katharine left the brewing house, and hurried to the barnyard, where two maids were wringing the necks of some fat hens. Then she went to the kitchen, to satisfy herself that everything was progressing in orderly fashion. Afterward, accompanied by Wolfgang and a man-servant, she walked through the still silent streets to an orchard, which Luther owned, in the neighborhood of the pig-market. Here, overshadowed by dense willow-bushes, lay a little fish-pond. The two men set to work, casting their net, and soon Katharine, who in the meantime had plucked a basket full of ripe pears, saw her tub filled with fish of various kinds.

" These will please the Doctor," she said, with a satisfied smile. " He is a great lover of fish, and this dish shall serve as a special ornament to our feast."

" With your permission," interrupted Daniel, the servant, " I have not yet been able to learn what is the occasion of this feast."

" Do you not know, Daniel, that we at last have peace in Germany?" asked Katharine, surprised. On the homeward walk she told him what had taken place at the diet at Nuremberg: that the protestant princes had agreed to furnish the Emperor with aid against the Turks, on condition that he would not further molest them in the exercise of their religion, but concede to the Gospel its rights, until the matter should be determined by a general church council.

As they entered the Court, master Peter, the barber, came hurriedly from the house, greeted Mistress Katharine, and asked if the Doctor were not at home. He had knocked three times at the study-door, without receiving an answer.

" No doubt," said Katharine, " he has been at his books all night."

She went to her husband's chamber,—his bed was

untouched; then she hurried to his study, and knocking repeatedly, heard no sound from within. She anxiously opened the door;—there sat the Doctor, motionless, bending over a book. Beside him on the table stood a plate with a piece of dry bread and half a herring.

"Doctor!" exclaimed Katharine, pausing at the door. Luther did not move. She went to him, took his hand, and bent over him, with a look of mingled anxiety and reproach.

Luther looked up in surprise.

"Dearest Doctor," said Katharine, "how you have alarmed me. Why do you do thus?"

Her question aroused him fully. A shadow passed over his face, and he pointed to the Hebrew Bible before him: "Why do you reproach me, Kate? think you that what I am doing is evil? Do you not know that I must work while it is day? For the night cometh, when no man can work."

He spoke almost harshly, but she knew that he was not angry. She silently caressed the kind hand, whose labors for the weal of the human race never ceased. Her eyes fell upon the half-consumed herring, and with a sad smile she said: "How is it that with such meagre fare you have so strong and stately a figure? Melanchthon appears as a lad beside you.—But to-day you must permit your wife to refresh you with a festive repast, after your labors. Our friends are coming to rejoice with us over the newly-won peace."

Luther passed his hand over his forehead. "I had well-nigh forgotten ; but I shall enjoy our feast in the company of my friends. Spalatin too has promised to be present." He rose, and laying his hand on his wife's shoulder, said gently : "My dear wife, how heartily you are concerned for me. Wish me joy that God has given me a helpmate, who so carefully watches over my health, and bears so patiently with my faults and infirmities. Dr. Martin would far ill, had he not his Kate, who is better able, than he, to rule his household."

Katharine was disconcerted by his praise, and to change the subject said : "Master Peter, the barber, is waiting ; may he come in, dear Doctor ?"

Luther nodded, and the barber—a small, lean man, with thoughtful eyes, and a nimble tongue—was admitted. He greeted the Doctor respectfully. While he was stirring the soap in the cup, Luther asked :

"Well, master, what news do you bring me to-day ?"

Peter was silent for a moment, then stammered : "Ah, most reverend Doctor, the newest is this, that master Peter has not yet learned how to pray. I have long desired to ask you, for, being a great theologian, you may well instruct a poor Christian in this art."

Luther smiled. "First do your work; afterwards I will tell you."

The barber made haste, impatient for his lesson to begin.

"Sit down, dear master Peter," said Luther, when he had finished. "You say praying is an art? Yes, verily,—an art, which the Papists little understand. And yet it is easily learned by every sincere Christian. See, master Peter, when your soul is disinclined to prayer, you must rouse it. Take your Psalter, withdraw to a quiet place, and read until your heart grows warm. You may also take your Catechism and devoutly consider the five Parts. This is an excellent means of kindling a flame within the heart. Although I am an old Doctor of Theology, yet like a child from its mother, I draw daily nourishment from the article of the Christian Faith and that of the Lord's Prayer. When you pray, let it be with a whole, undivided heart. Even a good barber must needs fix his eyes and his thoughts upon his razor, and not chatter and gaze about him."

Master Peter in many words expressed his gratitude, and rose to leave; but Luther detanied him, saying:

" If you have time, stay, and be present at our morning worship."

He took the Bible and Catechism from the table,
and, followed by the barber, proceeded to the great
hall, where the household was already assembled, and
awaiting the master's appearance.

After a pleasant greeting, all took their places at the
long, oaken table. Luther sat at the head ; at his right
Mistress Katharine with Aunt Lena and the children ;
at his left Peter and Jerome Weller, with Wolfgang
and four other young men, who were regarded as members of the family ; opposite them, the sisters Elsa and
Lena Kaufman, and at the lower end the servants.

Luther began with his full, rich voice, all the other
voices, deep and high, joining in, and reverently singing :

" In these our days so perilous,[1]
　　Lord, peace in mercy send us ;
　　No God but Thee can fight for us,
　　No God but Thee defend us ;
　　Thou, our only God and Saviour."

After the master of the house had read the 23d
Psalm, all rose and devoutly repeated the Morning
Prayer :

" In the name of the Father, Son and Holy Ghost.

[1] Translated by R. Massie.

Amen. I give thanks unto thee, Heavenly Father, through Jesus Christ Thy dear Son, that Thou hast protected me through the night from all danger and harm; and I beseech Thee to preserve and keep me, this day also, from all sin and evil; that in all my thoughts, words, and deeds, I may serve and please Thee. Into Thy hands I commend my body and soul, and all that is mine. Let Thy holy angel have charge concerning me, that the wicked one have no power over me. Amen." [1]

"Now let us hear the catechism," continued Luther. "Wolfgang, will you begin?"

Wolfgang rose, with folded hands, and recited the first commandment; his neighbor the second and so on, until it came to Luther's turn, who like the rest, repeated his portion.

"Dear Hans," Luther asked his six-year-old son, "can you tell me where I ended my explanation yesterday?"

"At the close of the ten commandments, dear father," was the ready answer.

"Then give heed," said Luther, "that you may know what is meant by ' the law.' The creature may well fear the law, with its threats and penalties. It is God's purpose, that the law should cause sinners to

[1] Church Book, Catechism, p. 55.

tremble ; for it is a taskmaster, holding the scourge in
his right hand. But understand me well,—the law is
not a taskmaster for its own sake, as though it delighted
in punishment, but it is evermore pointing to Christ.
What manner of master would he be, who tormented
and chastised his scholars without ceasing, yet taught
them nothing ? Of such schoolmasters there have been
many,—tyrants, who made their schools places of torture, beating without reason or measure the poor
children, who studied with great labor and diligence,
and yet with small profit. The law is a master of
quite another sort, not only making its children to fear,
but driving to Christ those who fall under its condem-
nation. But having driven us to Him, threats no longer avail. Were Moses to accuse my conscience, I
should say : Nay, Moses, but Christ is here. And on
the blessed Judgment Day, Moses will say to me :
Thou hast understood me well. For he that is in
Christ, is delivered from the law, as the Scripture
saith : ' Christ is the end of the law.' Those who are
Christ's, are no longer under the law, but are sanctified." Turning to his wife, he said suddenly : " Dear
Kate, do you believe that you are sanctified ? "

Taken aback by his abrupt question, she was unable
at once to reply. After considering for a moment,
she said : " How should I believe that I am sanctified ?
Am I not a great sinner ? "

The Doctor smiled. "See the popish unbelief,—
how it has wounded the hearts of men, and possessed
the inner nature so entirely, that it sees nothing beyond that outward, personal righteousness and holiness,
which we achieve for ourselves. Dear Kate, if you
believe that you are baptized a Christian, you must
needs believe that you are sanctified. Holy baptism
has power, so to change our sinfulness, that although
continually present and felt, yet it does not condemn
us."

A faint blush rose to Katharine's cheek, and a mute,
eloquent glance thanked her husband for his comfort-
ing words.

Thereafter, following the master's example, all rose
while he pronounced the blessing. The maidservants
then brought in the morning meal, which was eaten in
silence ; after which all went to their work.

The Doctor brought from his study the Hebrew
Bible and, accompanied by Peter Weller, repaired to
the University, to lecture upon the Book of Genesis.
Jerome took Hans to his own room, where he instruct-
ed the child in reading and writing.

During the forenoon a long table, covered with a
fresh linen cloth, was placed in the court-yard, under
the pear-tree ; the Doctor had desired to enjoy this
festive occasion under the open sky.

But darker rose the clouds, driven by a strong wind, and soon the first heavy drops plashed upon the ground. Katharine called her maids, to remove the table, and complained to her husband, who had just returned, that the rain was spoiling her pleasure.

"Not so, dear Kate," protested Luther. "God gives us what is worth many hundred thousand florins. It is now raining wheat, oats, corn, grass, and the like, for which we should thank the dear Lord, and not murmur. There is abundant room within the house, —Hark! Is not that a wagon? It is surely Spalatin. I feared he might not come. The other guests are already here."

A wagon rolled into the court, and a moment later, in the pouring rain, Luther held his beloved Spalatin in his arms. The other guests hurried from the house to greet the new comer—Melanchthon, Jonas, Bugenhagen, George Rörer, the chaplain of St. Mary's, Kaspar Cruciger, and Lucas Kranach. The wives of Jonas and Melanchthon had also been invited. Both were namesakes and warm friends of Mistress Luther, so that on that day three Katharines sat at table together.

Luther's friends rejoiced to see his cheerful mood, for only lately his spirit had been oppressed by deep melancholy. He inquired with much interest after

the health of the Elector, who had been ailing since
February, and the favorable report which Spalatin
was able to give, added to the general cheerfulness.

After much pleasant talk, Luther rose from his chair,
lifted his glass, and said: "My dear friends, it has
hitherto been the custom among Christians, to cross
themselves at the mention of the Infidel, and to wish
him much evil, as the enemy of God and the spoiler
of Christendom. But to-day it is more fitting that we
thank·him and drink to his health."

The men laughed at the jest. The Sultan Suleiman
had indeed been the means of bringing about a peace
between the Emperor and the allied Protestant princes. The danger which threatened the German Empire from the east, had compelled him to purchase
their aid against the common enemy, by yielding to
their demands in the matter of religion.

Luther continued : "Every creature becomes, often
unwittingly, an instrument in the hand of God, for
the accomplishing of His holy Will. Those who plan
to do evil, do good instead; and while they would
fain destroy God's kingdom, they help to build it up.
May our faith never grow weary, for the Lord has
many ways and means, even where our short sight can
see no remedy. Here the Infidel himself must needs
help the Gospel, in despite of the Pope and the Em-

peror.—How mercifully the Lord has sustained his cause ! Everywhere throughout the Empire there are many who follow the truth. The building is under roof; it now needs to be completed and preserved. A new generation has arisen. The burden no longer rests upon me alone ; but many stand as pillars of the new life, as leaders in the warfare between darkness and light."

Spalatin nodded : "Yes, Brother Martin, I too rejoice in the advancement of the good cause. The Elector returned with renewed hopefulness from Nuremberg, which has doubtless contributed to the improvement in his health."

" I have taken a hearty draught in honor of the Turk," said the chaplain Rörer, " but far greater honor is due to the man, whose wisdom brought about the peace between the Emperor and the Union of Smalcald ;—the man who so clearly distinguishes between what is God's and what is Cæsar's ; better than Zwingli, whose mingling of spiritual with temporal things has caused his destruction."

Luther, towards whom, at these words, all·eyes were turned, lifted his hand, and said earnestly : " Dear Rörer, you know that such praise pleases me little. What I am, I am by the grace of God,—to Him alone the honor is due."

Spalatin, in the meantime, was whispering into Katharine's ear : " His grace, the Elector, sends your husband through me a gift of a hundred gold florins. Small as it is, in comparison with the consolation he received from Dr. Luther during his recent illness, yet his heart urged him to show his gratitude, as far as he is able. I will not offer it to the Doctor, knowing that he will refuse the gift, which I pray you, dear Mistress Luther, to accept ; for I know that you have need of it, and the Elector will be much pleased."

Katharine whispered her thanks and said : "It is impossible to change the Doctor's mind in these matters. Only the day before yesterday, a young man who had finished his studies, and lacked the money for his homeward journey, came to us for help. My husband reached into his pocket, and finding it empty, he took a silver cup from the shelf and offered it to his student, who refused to accept it. I made signs to the Doctor with my eyes ; but as though he neither saw nor heard, he crushed the cup in his strong hand, and forced it upon the young man, saying : " I have no need of silver cups. Take it to the silver- smith, and whatever he gives you, is yours."

Spalatin's eyes glistened, as he glanced toward Dr. Martin, and with admiring veneration, he said softly : " That is Luther ! "

Presently, Katharine rose, and brought in the fish. When in passing it around, she came to her husband, he tapped her on the shoulder. "Kate, I think you have more pleasure from your small fish-pond, than many a nobleman from his large ones, whence he can draw hundreds of fish. Ah, many an one lives in plenty, and yet cannot enjoy God's gifts with profit and pleasure."

Melanchthon, as was his habit, had sat in silent meditation. Suddenly he looked up, and turning to Luther, said: "I marvel, what our enemies would say if they saw us sitting thus pleasantly together?"

"Let them say what they will," interrupted Luther. "If we fast, they cry: Pharisees and hypocrites. If we eat, they say: Gluttons and wine-bibbers! Thus it was when our Saviour lived upon the earth. But what says our Lord in Heaven, when we enjoy His gifts? Truly, He has made them all for our use, and asks nothing further, than that we acknowledge them as His gifts, and receive them with thanksgiving."

The conversation continued for an hour longer; then Luther and his friends rose and gave thanks after meat.

The air having grown cool and fresh after the rain, the men repaired to the court, to enjoy a game of bowls, while the women sat down together under the pear-tree.

The friendship of these three women was not less intimate than that of their husbands; especially were Katharine and the wife of Justus Jonas congenial, sharing joy and sorrow with one another. Often, when Luther's forebodings pointed to an early death, and his imagination pictured to him his widowed wife, he referred her to Mistress Katharine Jonas for support and consolation. The mothers' friendship had descended to the children, who were fond of playing and studying together.

Suddenly Luther's voice was heard, welcoming a new guest, and looking up, they saw John Walter, the choir-master from Torgau, whom Luther held in high esteem. There were joyous greetings from all, except Wolfgang, who was ill pleased at the interruption, and grumbled to himself: "Why must he come upon us just at this moment? Now the game is at an end, and so forth, and the miserable singing and howling will begin." The worthy Wolfgang, who had doubtless taken his lessons in singing from the jackdaws and magpies, considered a game of bowls superior to the finest music.

His fears were speedily realized. All gathered around the choir-master, and under his direction song after song was sung,—first folk-songs, of which Luther was very fond, then hymns and chorales, such as at Luther's request and with his assistance Walter had published for the Protestant worship. Higher and higher rose their spirits upon the wings of song, until the enthusiasm reached its climax, as Walter intoned that glorious song of battle and triumph : "A mighty Fortress is our God." The sounds re-echoed from the convent walls, and the evening wind bore the triumphal strains forth into the streets of the town. Wondrous was the power of this heroic song, which, with its majestic waves of sound, seized upon every heart. Even Wolfgang yielded, and added his croaking voice to the chorus.

The twilight slowly gathered, and after Katharine had offered her guests a light refreshment, all, except Spalatin and Walter, returned to their homes.

CHAPTER XVIII.

WITTENBERG, in the 16th Century, was a wretched town. The houses, built of wood, were thatched with straw. The narrow, crooked streets were paved roughly, or not at all; and in rainy weather, or during the spring thaws, became almost impassable. A few prominent buildings,—the fine churches, the Elector's palace, the University, the Franciscan and Augustinian convents, and the dwellings of some wealthy citizens, alone raised it to the dignity of a town.

The surrounding country had been meagerly dealt with by nature. Luther was wont to say: "Land,—thou art nothing but sand!" In every direction stretched wastes of sand. In the immediate neighborhood of the town, however, especially toward the South, where rolled the yellow waters of the Elbe, occasional clumps of trees, and even vineyards were to be seen. Here many citizens of Wittenberg had planted charming gardens, whither they went to refresh themselves during the heat of summer.

One garden especially, which lay near the Elster-gate, gave evidence of artistic skill and careful culture. The shrubs and flower beds were tastefully arranged. A little pond, fed by a spring, lay hidden among rustling reeds ; and in the midst of a large gravelled space rose a white summer house.

One bright day in the Summer of 1534, a merry little company was gathered here. A strong, active boy of nine, was the leader in their games, and their occasional excursions to the strawberry-beds. It was his birthday, and by reason of this circumstance, and of his seniority, he ruled over the younger ones,— a gentle little maiden of six, and two boys, of two and four.

Within the Summer-house sat the mother, holding a baby in her arms, and watching the play of her children,—now and then calling out a word of warning, when the merriment grew too boisterous, or when the eldest insisted too vigorously upon his rights.

It was Katharine, who after her day's work had come with her children to this favorite spot,—here, under the open sky, and among the flowers, she wished to celebrate the day on which, nine years ago, God's grace had given her her first-born son.

Luther might well say, with the Psalmist: "My wife is as a fruitful vine by the side of my house ; my children like olive plants round about my table,"—

five healthy, happy children they were ; and the mother still fresh and blooming, as though sorrow could
not touch her.

Suddenly a shout arose: "Aunt Lena! Aunt Lena
is coming!" and the children sprang towards the old
woman, as though she were a fortress, to be carried by
assault.

They were very fond of the good aunt, who always
had time and patience to answer their endless questions, who told them such lovely tales in the twilight;
who dressed Lena's dolls, and made soldiers of paste-
board for the boys, and never betrayed their childish
wrong-doings to father or mother. But to-day their
enthusiastic greeting was largely mingled with self-inte-
rest. They wanted her to take charge of the little
Gretchen, that their mother might play with them ;—
this being a great favor, and a rare one, for the mother's hands were always busy. Aunt Lena, being a
person of much penetration, guessed their wishes, and
did her part most willingly.

They played hide-and-seek and blind man's buff.
They counted the peas in the pods, by holding them
up to the light, and there was much laughter among
the boys, at their mother's failures. She herself felt
light-hearted and strong,—were not her children in
good health,—and the Doctor well, and vigorously at
work upon his new book?

But in time she wearied of the play and Wolfgang's appearance was a welcome interruption. He announced that the Doctor would probably not come before evening. Then from a basket he emptied a variety of buns and cakes upon the table, which quieted the noisy company for a time.

Hans seemed to have special business with Wolfgang. His eyes betrayed his eagerness; but Wolfgang seemed not to understand this mute appeal. When he found himself unobserved, he whispered: "Wolfgang, let us look after the bird-traps!" Wolfgang was not easy to persuade. He remembered the lecture he had received but the other day, when he presented the Doctor with a tame bullfinch. Luther told him sharply, that he took no pleasure in captive birds, which the Lord had not created to the end that Master Wolfgang Sieberger might snare them in his nets. But Hans pleaded so strongly,—it was his birthday, and Wolfgang yielded.

They stole away secretly. But Martin, the four-year-old, perceiving their intention, cried out after the fugitives, and wanted to be taken along. With many promises and persuasions he was finally pacified, and induced to remain behind.

Not far from the garden, near the University, was a secluded little copse, where multitudes of the feathery

tribe were wont to congregate.   It was here that Wolfgang had set his traps.   As they entered the grove, a
flock of finches rose into the air.   Their notes sounded
like mocking laughter to the bird-catchers, who
always came too late, and must needs be content, if
after a fortnight's watching, they snared a silly robin
or a saucy sparrow.   As a bird-catcher, Wolfgang had
small luck, at which he wondered greatly, for all his
measures were taken strictly according to the rules of
the craft, and the spot was well chosen for his purpose.   Perhaps the wood-nymphs spoiled his sport!
To-day again he caught nothing.   Finally, his patience was exhausted.   He sprang up and gave vent to
his feelings in a vigorous oath, which the echoes flung
back to him with derisive distinctness.

The sportsmen left the copse, in a bad humor.   As
they approached the garden, Wolfgang exclaimed, in
consternation : " The Doctor has come.   There will
be a fine reception for us, and so forth ! " and with
lagging footsteps they went to meet their fate.

Luther had arrived earlier than he expected ; and
finding Hans absent, at once suspected the truth.
Seating himself in the summer-house, he soon covered
a sheet of paper with writing.

He received the culprits with a stern look.   There
was no need of questioning them, their guilt was so

clearly written upon their faces. Wolfgang stammered something that sounded like an apology, but Luther interrupted him : " Sit here, Wolfgang ; and you, Hans, sit beside him ; and all the rest come hither, and hear the complaint, which has come to my hands.

When all were assembled, the Doctor read as follows :

" To our well-inclined friend, Dr. Martin Luther, Professor and preacher at Wittenberg. We thrushes, robins, linnets and other honest and peaceable birds, who are sojourning in these parts, would have you know that a certain Wolfgang Sieberger, your servant, has committed a daring and ruthless deed, in that, out of malice and hatred toward us, he has purchased dearly certain old and ragged nets, wherewith he purposes not only to snare our good friends, the finches ; but would fain deny to us also, who have in no wise wronged him, the liberty of flying in the air, and of picking up the grains which God has strewn for us. All this being, as you may suppose, a grievous oppression to us poor birds, we would direct to you our humble petition : That you restrain your servant from his evil design ; or, failing in this, that you command him, in the evenings to scatter grain upon this place, and in the morning not to rise before eight o'clock. If he consents, we will be content and even grateful to him. But if, on the contrary, he continues to persecute us, we will pray to the good Lord to punish him ; and we hope that some day he may find toads, and snails, and grasshoppers, instead of birds, in his net; and that at night the mice, fleas, and other vermin, shall cause him such torment, as to make him forget his evil designs against our liberty. Why does he spare the sparrows, magpies, jackdaws, mice and rats, which do you much harm, which rob and steal, carrying away your corn, oats and barley—while we seek only after crumbs and scattered grains, freeing you moreover from flies, gnats and other troublesome insects? We ask if this be just and reasonable? And we trust that in future we may rest undisturbed by his snares and nets.

"Given in our airy habitation among the trees, under our usual seal."

Without adding a word, without a glance at the accused, Luther folded the paper and put it into his pocket. Wolfgang's feelings were those of a convicted criminal, whose sentence is being read. He turned red and white, and would have been glad to slip away, had such an escape been possible.

Hans sat limp and dejected. He was plunged from his eminence as the hero of a birthday celebration! He waited eagerly for a lecture from his father, which would have relieved his conscience. But when he was passed by without a glance, and the father, with tender, loving words turned to the other children, especially to Lena, the gentle little daughter, his torture became well-nigh unbearable. With secret horror he remembered the time when, for a mischievous prank, he had been banished for three days from his father's presence, and all his mother's pleadings had been in vain. His father's words still rang painfully in his ears: "I would rather have a dead son than a disobedient one. It is not for naught that St. Paul says 'a bishop shall rule well his own house, and have his children in subjection,'—that he may set a good example, and not become an offense to other people."

Hans would have wept, but inward fear dried up the source of his tears, and he was denied the relief of turning his trouble into water. At supper he was unable to swallow a morsel; and his father's kind words to the others pierced him like a knife. Lena sat very still;—now and then her eyes wandered toward her brother,—his sorrow was hers. On a former occasion Luther had said to his wife: "If one would see a living illustration of the Saviour's words: 'Rejoice with them that do rejoice, and weep with them that weep,' one needs but look at our little Lena. She has a fine, sensitive soul, like an Æolian harp, that sounds and sings, if but a breath of air touches its strings."

After supper, Lena clung to her father, caressed his hand, and looked up into his face with a wistful smile.

"What would you have, my Lena?" asked her father gently, lifting her upon his knee.

"It is Hans' birthday!" she whispered, and two great tears filled her soft, blue eyes. Her father, touched by her loving heart, folded his little daughter in his arms and kissed her forehead. He beckoned to Hans: "Come hither, thou sinner, thy intercessor has conquered my heart, so that I must needs have pity on thee!"

Hans would fain have shouted for joy, but he restrained himself, and pressing close to his sister, he whispered: "Lena, you shall have my clapper-mill for this!"

Luther turned to his wife and Aunt Lena. "Here you may see," he said, "how powerful a mediator we have in our Lord Jesus Christ, whom the Heavenly Father cannot refuse, when He pleads for sinners. If my daughter thus speedily conquered my heart, how much more able is Christ to dispel the Heavenly Father's anger, that the sinner may go free. When I found this assurance in the Holy Scriptures, that we cannot be saved by our own virtue, but only by the merits and intercession of Jesus Christ,—a new life

was born within me, and I was constrained to pro-
claim it to all the world. I am heartily glad, and
thank the Lord, that the Bible has gone forth among
the German people, in the German tongue. Many à
drop of sweat cleaves to it, yet I labored with pleasure
and delight, for now all can see for themselves what
God's Word is, and wherefore the Saviour came into
the world.—I regard this work as the greatest of my
life ; and if God were now to call me hence, I should
willingly say : Lord, here I am."

Here the little, chubby-faced Paul, bestriding a
stick, came prancing along. In his haste he dashed
against his father, and was miserably overthrown.
Every one laughed at his discomfiture, but his father
lifted the little fellow upon his knee, and said : " Paul
must one day be a soldier, and ride against the Turks;
then doubtless Germany will have peace from that
quarter." He stroked the curly head, and turning to
Katharine, said : " How fondly parents cling to their
youngest children,—it is no doubt, because of their
helpless condition. Hans, and Lena, and even Martin can make their wants known,—but these little ones
cannot. Yet the love is the same toward them all."

Katharine held out the baby, Gretchen, and said
with a smile : " This one needs love more than any,
—and yet you do not mention her, dear Doctor."

Luther took the child in his arms and caressed it, saying: "There is a great sacredness about a little child, of whom the Scriptures say: 'Their angels do always behold the face of my Father who is in heaven.' I would give all the honor I have had, and shall have in this world, had I died at the age of this child. A child's life is the happiest: it has no temporal cares, knows nothing of the disturbers of the Church, has no fear of death or hell, but only pure and happy fancies. My dear little child, thou and all who are dear to me are hated of the Pope, Duke George, the Devil and all their friends. But the child is not disturbed, fears nothing, and laughs at their anger."

The Evening had come, and Katharine began to prepare for their return to town, the physician having strictly forbidden Luther to remain in the open air after nightfall. He seemed little inclined to exchange the fresh, pure air for the closeness of the narrow streets, but found himself unable to resist his wife's pleading. With a smile he submitted, saying: "Kate, you persuade me to do your will in all things!"

CHAPTER XIX.

RISEN FROM THE DEAD.

THE earth was already thickly covered with snow, yet the heavy, white flakes were still falling. The frost-flowers upon the windows hid the outside world from those within, and the footsteps in the streets sounded as though the ground were strewn with broken glass. Whoever could, stayed within doors.

Katharine was packing her husband's travelling trunk. He was about to undertake a journey. But it was not the thought of the distance, and of her own loneliness, that filled her eyes with tears, and her heart with anxious forebodings. He was ill, and she dreaded the effects of this wintry journey upon his enfeebled body. She would have pleaded with him to remain at home, had not the Elector so urgently desired his presence at Smalcald, where, before the assembled Protestant princes and representatives, he was desired to read the articles he had prepared for submission to the General Church Council, to be held at Mantua.

It was on the first day of February, 1537, when

(191)

Luther, wrapped in warm furs, and seated in the carriage sent him by the Elector John Frederick, passed
out of the Elster gate. Not only Katharine, but many
a citizen of Wittenberg looked anxiously after the
traveller, secretly reproaching the Elector for asking of
the sick man a sacrifice, which might plunge the
whole Protestant world into sorrow and confusion.

The days crept slowly by to Katharine. Many
letters came to the house of the spiritual leader of
Protestantism; yet there was none in the well-known,
rugged handwriting, although Luther had promised to
send her tidings as soon as possible, especially if any
harm should befall him. Week after week glided by;
her fears were slowly stilled, and she began to thank
God for this new grace.

On the 2d of March, a messenger rode into the
court, bringing a letter from the Doctor. Fear seized
upon Katharine, and her trembling fingers were scarcely able to open the packet. Yes, there it was written,
in terribly plain characters, that her forebodings had
not deceived her. The letter was dated from Gotha,
the 27th of February, and ran as follows:

"Grace and peace in Christ! You will have to
hire other horses, if you need them, dear Kate, for
His Grace will keep yours, until he can return them
to you by Master Philip. I myself, leaving Smalcald

yesterday, came hither in the Elector's coach. The reason is this,—I have been ill; rest and sleep forsook me, and food and drink sickened me. I was as one dead, and had commended you and the little ones to my dear Lord, thinking I should never see you again. I was sorely grieved for you,—yet I was prepared for the end. But so many prayers were made in my behalf, that they have prevailed, and I feel as one newly born. Therefore give thanks to God, and tell Aunt Lena and the children, to thank the Father in Heaven, for without His mercy they had surely lost their earthly father. The good prince endeavored by all means to procure me relief, but in vain. Neither did your remedy against indigestion do me any good. It is God alone who has done, and still does wonders for me, through the intercession of godly persons.

"This I write you, thinking that His Grace may have given orders to have you brought to meet me, that, in case I died upon the way, you might once more see me and speak with me. But there is no longer any need of it, and you can remain at home, God having helped me so abundantly that I hope soon to return to you in good health.

"To-day we are at Gotha. I have written you four

13

times, and am surprised that nothing has reached you.

"MARTIN LUTHER."

"*Tuesday after Reminiscere, 1537.*"

With tear-dimmed eyes Katharine read the letter, and then broke out in passionate lamentations, that she should be so far away from her beloved husband, when he most needed her care. She pictured to herself his sufferings, which her imagination painted in colors more somber than the reality. Full of her sorrow, she forgot to thank God for what He had done, until Aunt Lena reminded her of her duty.

"He wrote me four letters, and I received none of them," she complained. "Oh, how he must have longed for his wife and children. Yet none but strange faces were around him, and strange hands ministered to him. No doubt, they were kind and faithful, but his friends are not the same as his wife!"

She felt like a captive, and would fain have taken to herself wings, and hastened to him, whom her soul loved. Aunt Lena's arguments were without effect; and indeed, her uneasiness was but the instinct of an anxious heart. Through the magic tie of love, the souls of husband and wife were so linked together, that each in a measure felt the other's pain. Katharine's torturing anxiety, nowithstanding the reassuring tone of the letter, was but the premonition of further trouble. A relapse again brought her husband to the brink of the grave. It seemed to her as though he were stretching out his hands, and crying : " Come hither, and help me ! "

She was not deceived. At Gotha Luther again lay sick unto death. Beside him stood Bugenhagen, and administered the Body of our Lord. Gathering up the last remnants of strength, the sick man said to his friends:

"I know, thank God, that I did right in storming the papacy with the Word of God ; for it is a slanderer of God, of Christ and the Gospel. Pray my dear Philip, Jonas, Cruciger and others, to forgive me, wherein I may have wronged them. Comfort my Kate, and tell her to accept this sorrow with patience, forasmuch as she has had twelve years of happiness with me. She has served me faithfully,—may God reward her ! You will care for her and the children, as far as you are able. My gracious prince, the Elector, said to me at Smalcald : ' Have no fear for your wife,—she shall be to me as my wife, and your children as my children.' And I trust in his promise, for he is a truthful man. Greet the deacons of our church, tell them to labor in God's name for the Gospel, as the Holy Spirit prompts them. I will not prescribe to them the manner and measure of their

labors. May the merciful God strengthen them and
all others, that they abide by the pure doctrine, and
thank Him for their deliverance from the Antichrist.
I have earnestly commended them to the Lord,—He
will preserve them. I am now ready to die, if it is
His Will. I commit my soul into the hands of the
Father and of my Lord Jesus Christ, whom I preached
and confessed here upon earth!''

Thus he spoke, waiting for death, and his voice,
feeble as it was, yet reached to Wittenberg and was
felt by the keen sense of love. Katharine's uneasiness became unbearable, her fears urging her to go to
him,—perhaps she might be able to save his life.

She hired a carriage and hurried to Altenberg, praying and pleading without ceasing. Spalatin met her
with the glad news: "The Doctor is coming,—he has
announced his arrival." And he read to her the
verses which he had received the day before:

"See Christ the Lord, my Spalatin,
In him who seeks a sheltering inn.
'Tis Luther, ill, would rest with thee,
'Till he to health restored may be.
Do so to Luther!—God regard thee—
As unto Him, God will reward thee.
Read in His word,—'tis written there:
'All of Christ's Body members are.'''

"Be comforted, dear Mistress Luther," continued Spalatin ; "it fares better with him, for Melanchthon has added a few verses, written in a merry vein."

Katharine's suspense was soon relieved ; her husband arrived on the following day. Although the disorder was not wholly cured, yet under her gentle care he soon regained his strength. She endeavored, with redoubled attention, to make up for what she had been unable to do before, and felt rejoiced when with a silent pressure of the hand, or a grateful look, the Doctor spoke his thanks.

When on Maundy Thursday the bells called the citizens of Wittenberg to the town-church, they once more beheld in the pulpit the well-beloved, familiar face, and again received from his inspired lips the words of life.

CHAPTER XX.

TWO MILES south of Leipsic, on the road which leads to Altenburg, lay, among green meadows and graln fields, a secluded little estate, named Zulsdorf. The buildings, overshadowed by great oaks, were in a ruinous condition, the leaking roofs and gaping wounds in the masonry crying out for repair. In the spacious court-yard stood three wagons, loaded with tiles and timber, sent by the Elector's orders. Carpenters and masons were already at hand, to repair the ravages of time, and to put the little vine-covered dwelling-house in a habitable condition.

A woman, going from room to room, was giving directions, and noting the progress of the work; she encouraged the workmen to industry, for soon, she said, her husband would arrive, and all must be in readiness. From the house she went into the stable, and inquired of the overseer into the condition of the fields; then she hastened to the garden, to direct the maids, who were at work there. Immediately adjoining the garden was a marsh, overgrown with bushes

(198)

and tangled vines. Here, four men were busily engaged in draining and filling the waste place with
good earth. These also received a passing visit and
words of encouragement.

. It was evident at a glance that this woman was no
farmer's wife. Yet it was easy to see that she ruled
with pleasure over her little domain. She looked
rather pale and wan, as though but lately risen from
a sick-bed,—but strong, joyous life beamed from her
eyes.

From the orchard near by were heard ringing,
childish voices. A little girl of twelve came running
to her mother: "Mother, help me. Paul will not
come down from the pear-tree; he has torn his jacket,
and Margaret is eating too many pears!"

"Paul is a wild fellow!" said the mother, following
her little daughter to the orchard, where punishment
was speedily meted out to the culprits; but of so mild
a nature, that the merriment was scarcely interrupted.

"Come into the house, children," she then said,
"and hear what the dear father has written from Eisenach;" and all together they repaired to the sitting-
room, which had already been made comfortable.

No doubt the reader has guessed that this busy mother is no other than Mistress Katharine Luther, and

probably wonders, through what means she came into this neighborhood.

A cousin of Luther's, and the former owner of Zulsdorf, had fallen into debt. Urged by Katharine, Luther took pity on him, and for 610 florins, lent him. by the Elector, bought the estate.

When he brought his wife the deeds of the purchase, her face beamed with pleasure. Life in the country had always been her secret desire; and her garden, her dairy and barn-yard, which for so many years had supplied the necessities of the large household, had become her pride.

Luther, too, was glad of the acquisition of this retired spot, seeing in it a sheltered home for his wife, when he should leave this world.

For a time it seemed as though God meant to provide for Katharine another resting place,—out yonder, where the peaceful dead lay sleeping in their silent chambers. Hitherto it had been her lot oftentimes to watch by her husband's sickbed,—now it was Luther, who knelt beside his suffering wife. The plague, which in the year 1539 again visited Wittenberg with renewed fury, had spared Luther's house. But in February of the following year, Katharine fell ill, and grew so rapidly worse, that the physician gave up all hope. But there is one remedy,—more potent than all the apothecary's drugs, and this remedy Luther knew well how to apply. The great master of the art of prayer lay upon his knees, and with his prayers wrested his wife from the grasp of death. On the 3d of March he wrote to a friend : "My Kate has recovered from her illness, which was nigh unto death. She again eats and drinks with appetite, and by means of tables and benches, she creeps about the house, and is once more learning to walk."

The purchase of Zulsdorf now seemed like an inspiration from on high. There, in the country-quiet, in the fresh, wholesome air, his dear Kate would regain her health and strength.

She hailed the proposition with grateful joy, yet she refused to leave, while her husband remained in Wittenberg. He was soon to go to Hagenau, on the Elector's business, and in loving forgetfulness of self, she made the preparations for his journey. After his departure, Katharine, with Lena, Paul and Gretchen repaired to Zulsdorf. John and Martin were obliged to stay behind, because of their studies, but obtained the promise, that they should follow, when their father returned from his journey.

Katharine had already passed several weeks in the pure air, and amid the congenial occupations of her country home, and felt so revived and invigorated,

that she was able to give her husband the most satis-
factory reports of her progress.

Luther's letters also were full of cheering news.
His faith had achieved another victory, and had
saved the life of his dear friend, Philip Melanchthon,
who on the journey to Hagenau, suddenly fell ill.
The famous physician Sturz, who had attended Luther
during his illness at Smalcald, stood helpless by the ·
sick man's bedside, when Dr. Martin Luther, that
hero of love and trusting faith, entered the room.

His heart misgave him at the sight of his friend's
glassy eyes and sunken cheeks, and he exclaimed,
"God preserve us! How has the Devil marred this
vessel of thy grace!" His fear endured but for a moment. He turned to the window, and with a loud
voice pleaded with the Lord, to spare the life of his
friend,—and the dying man was restored.

The rumor reached Zulsdorf; and soon after, a letter, dated the 10th of July, came from Eisenach,
containing the following: "Master Philip has again
returned from death to life. He still looks pale, but
is of good cheer; jests and laughs with us, and eats
with a hearty appetite. God be praised for His goodness! and do you also with us thank the dear Father
in Heaven."

A few days later, another letter arrived:

"To my gracious Mistress Katharine Luther, of Bora and Zulsdorf, my sweetheart. My dear Mistress Kate. This is to inform your grace, that we are all, thank God, in good health. We eat like Bohemians, yet with moderation; drink like Germans, also with moderation, and are of good cheer,. for our gracious lord Bishop Amsdorf, of Magdeburg, is our companion at table.—We have had such heat and drought, that day and night are well nigh unbearable. Come, thou blessed Judgment Day. Amen.

   "Your lover, MARTIN LUTHER."

In a third letter he announced his coming, and it was this one, which Katharine now read to her children:

"To the Lady of Zulsdorf, Mistress Katharine Luther, my love. To-morrow—Tuesday—we purpose to leave this place. The diet at Hagenau has accomplished nothing,—labor, and time, and money have been wasted. Yet, even though we have done little else, we have drawn Master Philip from the grave, and will bring him home in good health, if it be God's will. Amen.

I am not certain, whether these letters will find you in Wittenberg or in Zulsdorf, otherwise I would write you more fully. God bless you!

   "Your lover, MARTIN LUTHER."

Monday after St. James' Day, 1540.

The reading was interrupted by shouts of joy from the children. Only Lena's face was thoughtful and she said: "Dear father does not know where we are. How will he come to us?"

"Never fear, my child," returned her mother, "your father will not fail to find the way."

Three days later the children, who many times each day climbed the hill behind the house, from whence they could see a long stretch of the road, observed in the distance a cloud of dust,—a coach became visible, and in hot haste, they ran to meet their father, the two older ones mercilessly disregarding the little Gretchen, who in her hurry had stumbled and fallen.

Their shouts brought Mistress Katharine to the door. She saw her beloved husband, surrounded by the children, whom he had lifted into the wagon, and waved a welcome to him with her handkerchief.

With proud satisfaction she led the Doctor, who had scarcely been granted time to change his dusty traveling clothes, through her new kingdom, eager to show him all its glories. It took time,—for everything had to be praised and explained. Luther listened patiently, for her joy was his, and with undisguised admiration he said at last: "Dear Lord Kate, I perceive that you are well qualified to rule over your new realm, and I will not withhold my respectful homage. But more than the kingdom, does the king himself please me, who has such round, rosy cheeks, and such a fresh, cheerful spirit.''

In the sitting-room, the maids had in the mean time prepared a repast; and Luther proved to them that he had not exaggerated, when he wrote that he could eat like a Bohemian, and drink like a German. Even though, as was his custom, he ate and drank sparingly, yet his food and drink seemed to refresh him, and Katharine and the children listened with delight, as he related the incidents of his journey.

Interrupting his story, he suddenly said : ''An old heathen of Rome, who was so happy as to possess a Zulsdorf of his own beyond the city walls, said of it :

> '' *Ille terrarum mihi praeter omnes*
> *Angulus ridet.''*

'' Which, interpreted, means ' Of all the places on the earth, this one to me is dearest.' Thus would I also sing. The Lord is very good. He does above all that we ask or think. If we petition Him for a piece of bread, He gives us a whole field of grain. I prayed God to give me back your life,—He gave me that, and Zulsdorf besides, and an abundant, fruitful year. This is like Paradise, and makes my heart warm ! Truly, if after the heat and burden of the day, God grants me a season of rest at the end of my life, I would fain enjoy it here.   I feel each day, that my strength is failing, and that my life is drawing to a close.   When the time comes, I will yield the sovereignty to you, and you shall be my 'lord' Kate indeed, to whom I will become an obedient subject."

CHAPTER XXI.

LUTHER'S LAST WILL.

"MAN proposes—God disposes." He who had labored more than all the others, was not to enjoy the coveted rest. Much still remained for him to do. Amid ceaseless toil and endeavor, the great life was to reach its end. Many a hard road must be traveled, before he should hear the Master's well-beloved voice : ·'Well done, thou good and faithful servant,—enter thou into the joy of thy Lord."

Yet he was weary, and his thoughts were constantly fixed upon death. To the many loving questions of friends he had but one answer: "Old age has come upon me, which is unsightly, cold and dreary. The pitcher is carried to the fountain until it breaks. I have lived long enough, and now my desire is, that God grant me a peaceful end, and that my useless body be put beneath the earth among His dead, and furnish food for the worms. Methinks the days that are past, were better than those that are to come ; for it seems as though evil times were drawing near. God help His own. Amen."

When the Elector, in his loving anxiety, sent his court-physician to the ailing man, Luther thanked his gracious sovereign for the kindness shown to his old and worn-out body, and added: "I would have been pleased, had the dear Lord Jesus taken me from hence, for I am of little further use upon the earth."

It was not the despondency of approaching age, which caused him to take this gloomy view of events, —but rather the inspired, prophetic eye, which foresaw a troubled future. The present was already fraught with evil. The waves of political strife ran high. The relations between the Protestant and Catholic parties were strained to the utmost. In Wittenberg itself,— in the very city which had once been the torch-bearer of the Reformation, Luther was forced to censure the profligacy of the students; and had personally entered the lists against the jurists, and their perversion of equity. But the world's answer to his cry of anguish, wrung from a Christian conscience, and to the honest testimony of the champion of truth, was hatred and enmity. In their blindness, men forgot the debt which Christianity owed to Dr. Martin, and repaid him with insult and calumny. All this weighed upon the giant spirit, and made the thought of death most welcome to him.

In this mood he sat in his study one day, in the beginning of the year 1542, and wrote his last Will and

Testament. He was prepared for its departure,— now he would arrange his temporal affairs, and put his house in order.

The document unconsciously shaped itself into a testimonial of honor and gratitude toward his wife. It seemed as though her husband desired to fix finally, in imperishable words, the love and respect he had never wearied of expressing.

The Will, which is still preserved, runs as follows: "I, Dr. Martin Luther, do herewith set forth, in my own handwriting, that on this present day, and in virtue of this document, I bequeath to my beloved and faithful wife Katharine, during her life-time, and to use according to her own pleasure:

"Firstly. The estate of Zulsdorf, which I have bought and put in order;

"Secondly. For her dwelling, the Bruno house, which was bought in Wolfgang's name;

"Thirdly. The cups and the trinkets,—such as rings, chains, silver and gold coins, which may be worth altogether about 1,000 florins.

"This I do, Firstly, because as my pious, true and faithful wife, she has at all times given me love and honor; and has borne to me and reared by God's blessing five living children;

"Secondly. Because I desire that she assume and

14

discharge all my debts, (unless I pay them during my lifetime), which, as far as I know, amount to about 450 florins,—perhaps more.

"Thirdly and chiefly, Because I desire that she shall not receive from the children, but they from her ; and that they honor her, and be subject to her, as God has commanded. I have seen how the Devil, by means of evil tongues, incites children to disobey this commandment,—especially where the mother is a widow, and the sons take wives, and the daughters husbands. I hold that a mother is the best guardian of her children, and will not use her property to their hurt or injury, but rather to their profit and advantage, they being her own flesh and blood.

"If, after my death, she should find herself under the necessity, or otherwise prompted to take another husband,—for I cannot set a limit to God's Will,—I have the sure confidence that she will continue to be a faithful mother to our children, and justly share with them her inheritance.

"And I herewith humbly pray my lord, the Elector John Frederick, that his grace will kindly confirm and administer this my bequest.

"I moreover request my friends, that they bear witness to the innocence of my dear Kate, if evil tongues should seek to work mischief, as though she had withheld anÿthing from the children. I herewith testify that there is nothing beyond the cups and trinkets above enumerated. Everybody knows what has been my income from my gracious master ; there has not been a farthing beyond, save such gifts as are reckoned with the trinkets. Yet my small income has sufficed for the support of a large household, which I count as a great and peculiar blessing. The marvel is, not that there is a lack of ready money, but that the debts are so few. I make this request, because the Devil, having failed to destroy me, may seek by all means to molest my Kate, because she has been, and, thank God, still is, Dr. Martin's wedded wife. This is my earnest and well-considered wish.

" MARTIN LUTHER.

" Given on the Day of the Epiphany, 1542."

On the same day, Luther sent for his friends, Melanchthon, Cruciger, and Bugenhagen, to affix their signatures as witnesses to the document. It was not shown to his wife, the Doctor fearing to arouse the sadness which overwhelmed her at the thought of separation.

A heavy weight was lifted from his mind, after he had thus fulfilled his duty toward his wife and children ; and he was able, with greater fervor than ever, to say in his daily prayer : " I desire to depart and to be with Christ."

CHAPTER XXII.

LITTLE LENA.

IT is written that "we must through much tribulation enter into the kingdom of God," and that "whom He loveth, He chasteneth."

Martin Luther and his wife had already passed through deep waters of grief and sorrow,—he, the hero in spiritual warfare, leading the way, and she following, keenly alive to every trouble that assailed her husband. But the season of trials was not yet past,—they were still, by God's Will, to taste the bitterest pain that can afflict a parent's heart.

One day, as they sat together under the pear-tree, surrounded by their children, the conversation chanced upon the sacrifice of Isaac.

"Good God," said Luther, "what a heart-break it must have been to Abraham, when he was commanded to slay his only and well-beloved son Isaac! What a painful journey that was, to Mount Moriah,—doubtless he told his wife nothing about it. Truly, had I been in his place, I believe I should have withstood."

His wife answered with a sigh: "I cannot grasp

the thought, that God should require of us to sacrifice our own child.''

Her objection again brought Luther upon the right path: "Dear Kate, yet you can believe that God suffered His only Son, our dear Lord and Saviour, Jesus Christ, to die for us? There was none He loved more, in Heaven or on earth, than His Son;— and yet He permitted Him to be crucified for us. Would not human reason say that God had shown Himself more tender and fatherly towards Caiaphas, Pilate, Herod, and the others, than toward His only Son? Abraham surely believed in the resurrection of the dead, when he was required to sacrifice his son, concerning whom the promise had been given, that through him the Messiah should be born, as the Epistle to the Hebrews testifies.''

Katharine could not but admit that he was right; yet her eyes rested wistfully upon her children, at the thought that God might demand them of her.

This conversation was forgotten and the blooming health of her children reassured the mother's heart. Yet the angel of death was about to gather the fairest flower of them all.

One day in September of 1542, Lena, who was sitting at work beside her mother, grew suddenly pale and complained of great pain in her breast. The physician, who was summoned immediately, was unable to discover the seat of the disorder. He prescribed a potion ; but in spite of the remedy, the child grew rapidly worse.

Father and mother watched by her bedside, each questioning the other's eyes, as though seeking comfort, and then, in their utter helplessness turning to Him, Who alone can save from death.

The child suffered much pain, but she lay quiet and uncomplaining, only the twitching muscles betrayed her agony. Her face seemed to grow more beautiful at the approach of death, as though the pure soul were shining through its transparent garment of flesh. When Katharine, seeing the anguish, which she was unable to relieve, could not restrain her tears, Lena's sweet, pleading eyes seemed to say to her : Do not grieve !

One morning Lena raised herself in bed, and said to her father : " Dear father, I have a great desire to see my brother Hans. Will you not send to Torgau, and ask Master Krodel, to give him leave of absence ? He is diligent, and will quickly make up the lost time."

Luther tenderly stroked the cold forehead, and promised.

Two days later, Hans arrived. He did not know, why he was called home ; for in his letter to Master

Marcus Krodel, under whose instruction Hans was placed, Luther had begged him, not to mention Lena's illness, therefore great was the boy's alarm, when he saw his little sister thus changed.

Their meeting was touching, — even Luther, the strong man, turned away, to hide his tears.

From day to day the parents' hearts alternated between hope and fear. Katharine's anxious eyes sought to read the physician's face, dreading to put her question into words.

There was no lack of sympathy. All the friends of the family,—indeed, all Wittenberg, shared in their sorrow.

For two weeks, Katharine had scarcely slept, watching her child with the strength of self-forgetting love. But at last nature demanded her right. She sank exhausted upon her bed, and while sleep brought a few blessed hours of unconsciousness, her spirit was soothed with a lovely dream-vision. She saw her little daughter, radiant with light, floating upon a cloud, and two fair youths coming to lead the maiden to the marriage feast.

In the morning she related her dream to her husband, and added : "Nothing is impossible with God. I take my dream to be a happy omen."

Melanchthon, who was present, smiled sadly, and

when Katharine had left the room, he said: "Do you read the vision thus, dear Martin? I would not take from your wife her hope, but knowing that you have already yielded the dear child to the Lord, I will tell you, what I take its meaning to be. The fair youths are the blessed angels, who will lead the maiden into the heavenly kingdom, to the true bridegroom."

Luther bowed his head and clasped his hands. After awhile he said: "I love her very dearly, and would fain keep her, if it is our Lord's will; but if it pleases Thee, dear Father, to take her, I will gladly know her to be with Thee."

After Melanchthon had gone, Luther returned to the sickroom, and seated himself beside the bed. The child's eyes were breaking, and her skin was almost transparent.

"Magdalena, my little daughter," said her father, with quivering lips, "you are content to stay with your father here,—and also content to go to the Father above?"

Softly, faintly, came the answer: "Yes, dear father, as God pleases."

The mother was kneeling upon the floor, weeping, —her face buried in her hands,—she could not witness the child's death.

Luther sought to comfort her: "Dear Kate, remember, whither Lena is going. The lines have fallen unto her in pleasant places. She has a goodly heritage."

But in the face of the last struggle, his strength forsook him. He sank upon his knees beside the bed, and wept bitterly, crying aloud: "O Lord, have mercy, and end her suffering!"

And God's angels flew softly through the chamber, kissed the maiden's brow, and led her home, to the heavenly bridegroom.

.   .   .   .

Outside, upon the stairs, the other children were watching, silently holding each other's hands, when one of the maids, with tear-swollen eyes, came to them and said; "You have no longer a sister Lena!"

The children cried out, and stared in dismay at the messenger of sorrow. Paul sprang to his feet, and exclaimed angrily: "It is not true! She is not dead!"

"She is not dead!" repeated Gretchen, and rose to go to her sister. Then their mother came toward them, and in her face the children read the truth.

The house was very silent. Every one stepped softly, as though Lena were sleeping, and must not be awakened. And not only was Luther's house a house of mourning, but every household in Wittenberg grieved iu sympathy.

With a trembling hand the stricken father wrote to his friend Justus Jonas, who in the preceding year had removed to Halle:

"My dearest Jonas! This is to tell you, that my dear daughter Magdalena has been born again, into the eternal kingdom of Christ. We,—that is my wife and I,—should truly feel only joy and gratitude at this happy and blessed departure, by which our child is removed from the power of the flesh, the world, the Turk and the devil. Yet natural love so masters us, that we cannot submit without sobs and tears and much heart-breaking. For she had taken a strong hold upon our affections,—our gentle, obedient daughter—by her looks, her words and her behavior, in life and in death, —and even the death of Christ cannot wholly wipe away our grief. She was, as you know, of a sweet and gentle disposition, and well-beloved of all. Praised be our Lord Jesus Christ, who hath thus called and glorified her. Oh, that we, and all who are dear to us, might have such a death,—yea, and such a life! This I ask of God, the Father of all grace and mercy.   MARTIN LUTHER."

Then he sought in prayer the strength he needed, for what remained to be done. When he entered the death-chamber, the mother was kneeling beside her child, whom she had herself prepared for her last rest-

ing-place, and was placing a branch of rosemary between the cold fingers.

How fair and lovely she was, her sweet, little Magdalena. Even death could not mar nor destroy her
gentle beauty, which seemed only glorified,—as it will
be upon the last day, when the grave shall yield up its
prey, and what was sown in corruption, shall be raised
in incorruption.

On the third day, the mortal remains of little Lena
lay in her flower-strewn coffin, which, because of the
crowds of people, had been placed in the court under
the pear-tree. Luther pressed a last kiss upon the still
face. "Thou dear child,—it is well with thee! Thou
wilt rise again, and shine as a star,—yea, as the sun.
My spirit rejoices, but according to the flesh I am very
sorrowful; for parting is painful beyond measure. It
is strange,—to know that she is at peace,—and yet to
mourn!"

He thanked the people who had came to testify
their sympathy, adding: "Rejoice with me, for I
have now a blessed saint in Heaven. Oh! may we
all have such a death as hers!"

"Yes, Reverend Doctor," exclaimed a voice from
the crowd, "you say truly,—yet every one would fain
keep his own,"

Luther replied: "I am glad, that she is in Heaven;
my sorrow is all of the flesh."

Then Katharine, supported by Melanchthon's wife, tottered toward the coffin, to bid her child a last farewell. At the sight of her, the bystanders began to weep and lament aloud, and Wolfgang, who had also approached, turned away—he could not see the mother's grief.

Lena's grave was beside that of her sister Elizabeth, and for the second time, Wolfgang must needs force his trembling hands to fashion a cross, upon which Luther wrote these words :

> " I little Magdalen, sleep here,
>   I'm Doctor Luther's daughter dear,
>   In this small chamber I shall rest,
>   Till summoned forth with all the blest ;
>   Tho' born in sin, not lost am I—
>   As was decreed—eternally.
>   I live, and all is well and good :
>   Christ ransomed me with His own blood."

When Luther returned from the burial, he said to his wife. " Our little daughter is at rest, both in body and soul. We Christians should not murmur,—knowing that it must be thus, and being sure of eternal life : for God's promise, given through His dear Son, cannot fail.''

" Ah, you are a strong man," sighed Katharine ; " but a mother cannot so quickly master her sorrow,

and a woman's heart is a weak and timid thing. God
will have patience with me—I will not murmur."

"Weep freely, dearest Kate," said Luther, "therefore were tears given us, and God knows best, what
miserable vessels of clay we are. He remembers, that
we are but dust, and bears with us, that His strength
may be made perfect in our weakness. And consider
this: Time is short; in a little while we shall meet
again with rejoicing, and our joy no man taketh from
us."

She clasped her hands, lifted her sad eyes toward
Heaven, and prayed: "Yea, Lord Jesus, come
quickly."

CHAPTER XXIII.

ONCE MORE IN ZULSDORF.

THREE years had passed. To the loss of their child,
another sorrow was added. Soon after Lena's death, the
wife of Justus Jonas died. She was a good and noble
woman, Katharine's dearest friend; and it was to her,
Luther hoped, his wife might after his death, look for
comfort and support. Once more, Luther's house
was turned into a house of mouring. But in time the
wounds healed,—and sharp grief gave place to loving, tender memories.

The simple, peaceful life at Zulsdorf had done much
to restore the stricken hearts. Small and modest as was
their home, yet to the great man it was a paradise,
and to Katharine's contented spirit, a kingdom. Her
taste for improvements involved her in many a struggle with the Elector's dishonest officials, who sought
to draw their own profit from every delivery of building material. Yet these annoyances were as nothing,
compared with the delights of country life.

Again, we find her busy in her domain, assisting
Gretchen in wreathing the entrance with evergreens,

(222)

and in strewing fresh sand upon the paths.

It was a glorious morning in July. Sweet summer scents rose from the fields, the clear air rang with the song of birds and the chirping of insects, and all created things seemed full of the joy of life.

" They must soon be coming," said Katharine, her eyes scanning the distant road. But hours passed ; and it was already afternoon, when Katharine, from the garden, heard the sound of approaching wheels. She hastened to the court,—a wagon rolled in at the gate, and Luther and his son John alighted.

" Praised be God, we are here," exclaimed Luther, after the first greeting was over. " I feel like a mariner, who has reached a safe harbor, after the dangers and tempests of the sea. I thank the dear heavenly Father, that He has prepared this refuge for me. His mercy is with me evermore."

He seemed tired, and his face was pale and worn. After he had refreshed himself with a cup of milk and a piece of bread, he sat down beside his wife, and turning to John and Margaret, said :

" Go away for a little while, children ; I need rest."

He lay down upon a couch, and taking his wife's hand, looked long and earnestly into her face. " My dear wife," he said at last, " I have much to tell you, that will no doubt astonish you. I cannot continue in Wittenberg, and I have bidden farewell to the city, where I labored for seven and thirty years."

"Doctor," cried Katharine, in amazement.

Luther continued: "It was a difficult decision to make; but it must needs be. My heart has grown cold, and I cannot abide in a city, where disorder and lawlessness reign supreme; where none heed my voice, and even the theologians no longer stand firm. Among the young people the profligacy of former times has broken out again, and even honest maidens go about the streets, arrayed in an unseemly manner. The priests aid the disorderly doings, by favoring secret betrothals. It is my wish therefore, that you sell our house, and all that we possess in Wittenberg. It would be best for us to continue here at Zulsdorf, while I am with you ; and my salary, which the Elector will not withdraw, will assist in keeping the household. After my death the various elements in Wittenberg will not suffer you to dwell there. It were better, therefore, that the change were made during my life-time. On my journey hither, I learned many things, that made me weary of the town, and I will not return to it, unless it be God's Will. The day after to-morrow I wish to go to Merseburg, where our dear prince George of Anhalt is at present administering the bishopric. He has been found faithful beyond measure, not only attending diligently to the outward duties of his office, but preaching to his people from the pulpit. I will rather eat the bread of poverty hereafter, than torture my few remaining days with the sight of the misrule at Wittenberg, and lose the fruits of my toilsome life. They know nothing as yet of my determination, which was formed on the way. I will write to Bugenhagen and to master Philip,— they may make it known to the University."

While he spoke, Katharine moved closer to her husband. Her eyes brightened, as he proceeded. When he paused, she pressed his hand, and said : " Dearest Doctor, you are giving me a great pleasure. I have long wished that we might remain here, where it is so full of God's peace. Yet I fear, that they will not suffer you to rest, but will urge you back again into the struggle."

" Be at ease, dear wife," said Luther, " it shall be as God wills. I will write at once."

She brought him pen, ink and paper, and an hour later, he entrusted to the coachman, who had brought him, two letters, to be delivered on his return to Wittenberg.

Three happy, restful days followed. The quiet restored Luther's spirits. He noted with interest the well-planned improvements made by his wife; tasted

15

and enjoyed the various fruits, grown on his own trees, and addressed many a merry, jesting speech to his "lord" Kate. The affection and trustfulness of his laborers gave him much pleasure. He conversed with them in their own language, and they were greatly rejoiced at the kindliness of the great man, of whom they knew that he was the friend of kings and nobles.

After a few days he felt so refreshed, that he was able to set out upon the journey to Merseburg, in the carriage sent him by prince George. On the 2d of August, he accompanied the princely ecclesiastic to Halle, where the latter was to receive the rite of ordination at his hands. He preached in the Cathedral to vast crowds of people, and then proceeded to Leipsic, where men were longing to hear the words of truth from his lips.

When he returned to Zulsdorf, he found his wife in tears. Again, her forebodings had been verified. "Ah, dearest Doctor," she cried, "our joy is at an end. Here is a letter from the Elector,—it came yesterday."

Luther read the Elector's words of dismay and sorrow at his determination. The sovereign gave his solemn promise, if Luther consented to remain at Wittenberg, to use his influence in removing the causes of his complaints, whose justice he admitted. He

most urgently entreated him to desist from his purpose, which would have further disastrous consequen-
ces ; Melanchthon having declared that he would not
remain in Wittenberg, without his friend Martin.

Luther had scarcely finished, when a stir was heard
without. As he opened the door, Melanchthon and
the burgomaster of Wittenberg, Ambrose Reuter entered. They added their pleadings to those of the
Elector, and were, if possible, even more pressing.

Luther could not resist. "As God pleases," he
said resignedly, with a glance toward his wife, who
stood by the window, scarcely able to restrain her
tears.

It was like a triumphal procession, when on the
16th of August, Luther, with his wife and eldest son,
seated in the carriage sent him by the Senate of Wittenberg, entered the Elstergate. The better elements
welcomed the beloved teacher with jubilant delight ;
many of the erring ones repented, and those that remained incorrigible, were summarily dealt with by the
University and the municipal authorities. With inward satisfaction, Luther saw this return to better
things, a result to which he gladly sacrificed the
coveted rest ; as, all his life long, it had been the rule
of his thinking and acting, to forget himself, for the
welfare of others.

CHAPTER XXIV.

PARTING.

The storm raged furiously, dashing heavy masses of
snow against the windows. The rooks hid in the
crevices of the masonry, scarcely venturing forth in
search of their daily bread. Men whose business
forced them to go abroad, wrapped themselves in
their warm cloaks, which failed to defend them against
the piercing cold.

Mistress Katharine sat at home, with Margaret, her
youngest child. Her face was pale and care-worn,
and told of many sleepless nights. Anxiety for her
husband lay like a stone upon her heart; for again he
had been obliged to leave his home,—the man, now
old, feeble, and broken in health, for whom there was
to be no rest upon earth.

In October and December of the past year, at the
request of the counts of Mansfeld, he had journeyed to
his former home, to act as peacemaker between the
discordant factions. Now, he had gone for the third
time, and days of sorrow and anxiety had followed his
departure. Katharine had no peace. She sought the

seclusion of her chamber, to dwell in spirit with her absent husband, until the solitude grew unbearable. But when she saw in Margaret's eyes the reflection of her own fears, she again longed to be alone.

She knew that her husband was tenderly cared for by her three sons and their tutor, Ambrose Rudtfelt; but it was not within their power to stay the inclemency of the weather, nor relieve the pains which tortured him. And from her heart rose the passionate prayer: "Lord, if Thou wouldst but send the springtime, for Thy servant's sake!"

And behold,—the spring came!

The wind changed, the ice broke, and the snow melted before the warm breath of the south.

With a grateful heart, Katharine breathed the balmy air. The lark's trill overhead seemed to her the voice of an angel, bringing God's answer to her prayer; and her lips whispered: "Thou art the God, that doest wonders!"

The following day, she was able to add: "Thou doest exceeding abundantly above all that we ask or think!" A letter arrived, dated from Halle, which quieted her fears. Again she read the precious, familiar, jesting words, and knew that her husband was of good cheer. Gretchen was quickly called, to hear the letter read :

" To my dear, kind Katharine Luther in Wittenberg. Grace and peace in the Lord. Dear Kate: We arrived in Halle to-day at 8 o'clock, but did not go to Eisleben, having met a huge Anabaptist, with high waves and masses of ice, which overran the earth, and threatened us with immersion. Neither could we return, because of the Mulda, and must fain lie quiet here at Halle, between the waters. Not that we desire to drink them, for we have good Rhenish wine, and Torgau beer ; we have refreshed ourselves and are of good cheer, waiting for the Saale to spend its fury. The coachmen, and we also, fear to tempt God by venturing into the water, inasmuch as the Devil hates us, and we think it wiser to avoid misfortune, than to regret it afterwards ; nor do we deem it necessary, to give the pope and his servants cause for rejoicing. I had not believed it possible, that the Saale could cause such a disturbance, and that it would thus flood the stony roads. Had you been here, you would have advised us to do as we have done ; and for once, your advice would have been followed.

" God bless you, Amen !　　MARTIN LUTHER.

"Halle, on the feast of the Conversion
of St. Paul, A. D. 1546."

The joy caused by this letter was still fresh, when another followed, dated from Eisleben :

"To my dearest mistress Katharine Luther, Doctor of Zulsdorf, lady of the pig market, and so forth.

"Grace and peace in Christ, and my poor, old, worn-out love to you, my dear Kate. I was very faint on the road, as we neared Eisleben,—by my own fault. Had you been here, you would have said it was the Jews' doing; for near Eisleben we passed through a village, where many Jews are living. Perhaps it was they who attacked me with so fierce a blast; for as we reached the village, a cold wind blew into the carriage and upon my head, that it seemed as though my brain were turning to ice. This may have caused the dizziness. But I am now, thank God, well again, except that the fair women of this place give me much trouble.

"When the more important matters are arranged, I must see to it, that we take some measures with regard to the Jews. Count Albert does not favor them, and if it is God's Will, I shall help him from the pulpit. . .

"The day before yesterday, your sons went to Mansfeld, Hans having begged the others to go with him. I do not know what they are doing there. If it were still cold, they might be shivering ; but now that it is warm, they may do and suffer other things, as it pleases them. May God bless you and all the household. My greetings to all.

"MARTIN LUTHER, your old lover.
"*February 1st, 1546.*"

The letters which followed, written on the sixth, seventh, and tenth of February, brought good tidings, and relieved Katharine of all uneasiness. Luther jestingly thanked her, "the saintly mistress Katharine Luther, in Wittenberg," for her anxiety in his behalf, which kept her awake at night. He tells her that, since she has been thus troubling herself, a fire broke out near his chamber-door, which might have consumed him; and that furthermore, a great stone almost fell upon his head, by which he would have been crushed, as in a mousetrap. "I fear, if you do not cease from troubling, that the earth will open and swallow us, and the elements pursue us to our destruction. Do you pray, and leave the care of us all to God; for it is written: Cast thy burden upon the Lord, and He shall sustain thee."

Luther's last letter, of the 14th, brought great rejoicing to his family, "Father is coming! Father is coming!" shouted little Margaret, falling upon her mother's neck.

He has finished his work; he has reconciled the factions, and sent home a basket of trout, a gift from the Countess Albert, and his bodily suffering is less. Everywhere he received high honors, he says, yet he' longs to be at home, and hopes to reach it before the end of the week.

" Father is coming ! Father is coming !"

He came ; but his home-coming was not as the fond
hearts of his wife and child had hoped.

. . . .

Why are the bells tolling thus mournfully throughout the German land? What is the meaning of the
bitter tears, shed by the German people! Why does
the Elector's messenger stand sad and trembling at
the door of Luther's house in Wittenberg, fearing to
deliver to mistress Luther the letter he bears? His
heart is well-nigh breaking,—he brings her the message, that since yesterday, she is a *widow*—her children *orphans !*

. . . .

A long and mournful procession moved along the
road from Eisleben. They were bringing the man
of God, who had journeyed to his old home, that
his birth-place might also become the place of his
death. Behind the heavy, leaden coffin followed a
stream of mourners. All had lost a beloved father,—
all were orphaned by his death. From every church-
tower the brazen tongues sent forth their last farewell
In the villages the peasants left their work, put on
their holiday attire, and in silence received the procession ; from the city gates, the clergy, the Senate, the
people and the schools, chanting psalms and hymns,

came forth to meet the sad convoy.

As they approached Wittenberg, its streets grew silent and deserted, for all the people had hastened out upon the road leading to Pratau.

In her lonely chamber sits a widow; her hands lie folded in her lap; her eyes are red with weeping; she is weary—oh so weary. Her heart is exhausted; she can scarcely grasp a thought; and like a blessed gift of God, a dull apathy has setttled upon her spirit, and blunted her grief. Her husband is dead, and she could not be at his side, at the supreme moment. If, by God's counsel, she was destined to lose him, must she be denied the last consolation of ministering to him, and closing his eyes?

She sat still,—unknowing, unheeding, overwhelmed by her great, unspeakable grief!

Hark! the bells are tolling! The people are streaming into the streets!

She rose and pressed both hands to her head.

The faithful Wolfgang entered, pale and trembling. Scarcely restraining his sobs, he took her hand.

"The Doctor is coming,—let us go to meet him!"

Katharine suffered him to lead her. She saw nothing of the surging crowd. The world was blotted from her sight,—all, save the coffin that held her husband's clay, and was followed by an endless procession of lords and noblemen on horseback, professors, students, senators, and countless multitudes of men, women and children, all weeping and lamenting aloud

She was led to a little carriage that had been provided for her, and thus she followed her beloved husband, whose face she was never again to see upon earth.

The procession moved toward the Castle-church, and entered the door, upon which, twenty-nine years ago, the hands, now cold in death, had nailed the ninety-five theses, and the blows of whose hammer re-echoed throughout Christendom. Justus Jonas, who in Eisleben had spoken before the open coffin, preached the funeral sermon on 1 Thess. 4: 13–18. His words were scarcely heard amid the sobs and cries of the people. Melanchthon, in the name of the University, then delivered a latin address, and the remains of the prophet of God sank into their last resting place at the foot of the altar.

. . . .

Katharine looked on. Her heart was empty. She had no tears.

When all was over, Melanchthon, the faithful, took her by the hand, and led her to her home, now so silent and desolate. He sought to comfort her, but his words seemed cold and powerless, over against such sorrow as hers.   She found her children and her household. awaiting her.   When they saw her, they broke out into fresh lamentations.

Then God sent her help.   In the face of the uni-versal mourning, her heart awoke to renewed trust in God ; and with glowing eyes and uplifted hands she cried : " My flesh and my heart faileth ; but God is the strength of my heart, and my portion for ever."

BOOK THIRD.

KATHARINE VON BORA;

THE WIDOW.

(237)

CHAPTER XXV.

ALONE.

THE woman who, for her husband's sake, might with reason have looked for exemption from the common fate of widowhood, was made to experience to the full the dreariness of her condition, and the world's ingratitude. But mankind is subject to the universal law, that "we must through much tribulation enter into the kingdom of God;" and the question is silenced, which involuntarily suggests itself: Lord, why hast Thou dealt thus severely with poor Katharine?

One day an official of the Elector's chancery knocked at the door of the chancellor, Dr. Brück, in Wittenberg, and after considerable delay and much formality was ushered into the presence of the distinguished man.

Dr. Gregory von Brück was of a tall and imposing stature. His fine features and lofty brow betokened a keen and vigorous intellect, and his brilliant, expressive eyes gave evidence of great mental activity. It was he who, at the diet of Augsburg, together with his colleague, Dr. Baier presented to the Emperor the

(239)

Confession of the Lutheran faith ; and from that day
forward his power and influence had steadily increased.
He was a frequent visitor at Luther's house, and although the cool reserve which the chancellor always
maintained toward Katharine, annoyed the Doctor,
yet it did not prevent him from doing justice to the
merits of his friend.   Luther never asked the reason
of the chancellor's behavior.   Had he done so, the
other would doubtless have learned better to appreciate
the wife of the great Doctor.

"What is your wish?" Brück demanded of the
counselor, who, bowing with great deference, replied :   .

"His grace the Elector, sends you his greeting, and
desires that you will give your opinion regarding the
affairs of Dr. Luther's widow, his Grace trusting that
you, as Luther's friend, will prove yourself a defender
and protector of this widow."

Brück's eyes assumed an impenetrable expression,
while his white hands toyed with a pen.

The counselor paused for a reply, and then continued : "You doubtless know, that she has sent a
petition to his Grace ! "

"A petition?" interrupted Brück, glancing sharply toward the speaker.   "It was so rumored ; but in
this matter she has not confided in me.   Do you know

the contents of the petition?"

"I know them," was the answer, "and it was to learn your opinion in the matter, that his Grace sent me hither."

"Say on!" urged the chancellor.

"You probably are aware," the counselor began, "that during the life-time of Dr. Martin, the Elector presented him with a capital of 1,000 florins, of which he enjoyed the interest during his later years. To this,—out of pity toward the family, and out of gratitude for the reformer's great services—his Grace desires to add a second thousand, to relieve somewhat the widow's needy condition. She has in her petition requested, that the promised 2,000 florins be invested in land, which yields a better income. She says further that the estate of Wachsdorf, adjoining her own estate of Zulsdorf, is for sale, that her late husband admired it, and that it can be bought for 2,000 florins."

The chancellor moved impatiently upon his seat. "This is a bad beginning. Does the woman dare to approach the Elector with a falsehood! Would she have it appear, that her husband coveted the land? I perceive her meaning. She is not satisfied with Zulsdorf, but must needs have a larger estate to manage and rule. If the Elector does her will, she will begin

16

to build and make improvements in Wachsdorf, as she did elsewhere, and will waste much money. Moreover, Wachsdorf is an unprofitable possession,—it is well known, that each spring the fields are flooded by the Elbe."

The counselor shook his head. "Pardon me, sir chancellor; I am well acquainted with Wachsdorf, having often been there in my youth, and I never heard of the disadvantage you mention. I hold it to be cheap at 2,000 florins, and the widow no doubt desires to possess it, for her children's sake."

The chancellor's face flushed, and he harshly exclaimed: "Her children? It is chiefly for their sake, that I oppose the purchase. For what will follow? The boys will waste their time with riding and bird catching, instead of sitting at their books. Mistress Katharine is very weak with her children, and unable to oppose them. It would be well therefore, if the boys were taken from her, and placed with competent tutors. But she is stubborn and refuses this, even as she refused my well-meant offer of giving Hans a position in the Elector's chancery. Her obstinacy will make it difficult to find guardians, every one knowing that he will have a hard time with the woman. I fear, moreover, that her ambition and avarice will prevent her from acting justly by her children, especially if, as I expect, she marries again."

"O sir," exclaimed the counselor indignantly, "how can you entertain such suspicions against a poor widow, of whom others speak very differently."

The chancellor lifted his hand: "Do not excite yourself. What you know, is from hearsay,—I have known her during many years of intercourse with her husband."

"I know her better than from hearsay" replied the other, "I read the Doctor's last will and testament, which he wrote in 1542, and which was submitted to his Grace for confirmation. From this document it is evident that Luther, who surely knew his wife better than any, trusted her entirely. Methinks the Elector has sent me to the wrong man,—to the widow's accuser rather than her defender. His Grace expected other things from you, and I would gladly be excused from carrying your message to him."

Brück rose from his chair, and excitedly paced the room, then suddenly pausing before the counselor, he said in a gentler tone: "You misunderstand me, and do me injustice in thinking me unfriendly toward Mistress Luther. I assure you, that I am only concerned for her welfare, although my advice may displease her. But I will relieve you of your duty, and write to the Elector myself."

The counselor breathed a sigh of relief: "Accept my thanks therefor, sir chancellor. May God give you wisdom to do the right, and a merciful heart toward the poor widow, whose lot is more pitiable than any other. Remember the old saying: "The widow's tears must needs flow, but they cry out against him who calls them forth."

The chancellor, slightly frowning, turned his eyes upon the other with a questioning glance, and dismissed him.

Then he wrote his report to the Elector.

Meanwhile, the counselor was sitting with the widow of the reformer, to form, if possible, his own opinion. He met there Master Philip Melanchthon, and remained three hours. From the heartiness with which he took leave of Mistress Katharine, it may be supposed that he was favorably impressed by what he saw and heard.

Two days later, he was summoned to the Elector, whom he found sitting at his writing-table with a letter in his hand.

"I expected you yesterday, dear Veit," said the Elector, "I wished to hear from your lips the view taken by our chancellor Brück, regarding the petition of Dr. Luther's widow. In the mean time I have received this letter, in which the chancellor gives his opinion more circumstantially. It has surprised me greatly, being written in a tone, that is far from friendly to the widow of our dear Doctor. He surely knows her well, having been much in Luther's house; and I must needs believe him, although I had imagined Doctor Luther's wife to be a very different woman."

With a bow, the counselor said : "Will your Grace permit me to give my opinion?"

"Say on, dear Veit," urged the Elector, leaning forward to listen.

The counselor began : "Master Brück is a highly learned man, and of great ability, which none will dispute. He has a clear eye in discerning the nature of things in general ; bnt here his judgment is at fault. He does injustice to the widow of Dr. Martin, and esteems her less highly than she deserves. I went to her myself, wishing to know her personally; and what I saw, and what Melanchthon told me, convinces me, that the chancellor is in error. I therefore pray your Grace, not to lay too much weight upon his communication, but to grant the widow's petition."

The Elector held out his hand : "I thank you from my heart, dear Veit. You have done me a great service," and the counselor withdrew. When the Elector was alone, he re-read the chancellor's letter.

Then, lifting his eyes to a portrait of Luther, which hung upon the wall opposite, he exclaimed : " No, posterity shall not accuse me of faithlessness ! Martin, thou glorified spirit, I promised thee with hand and lips, that thy wife and thy children should be to me as my own, and I will keep my promise. Even though thy wife were undeserving, yet, for thy sake, I would help her. Who could worthily repay thee, thou benefactor of mankind, the fountain, from which shall spring life and blessing to generations yet unborn ! "

.   .   .   .

In the Luther-house at Wittenberg, sacred henceforth to grief, Mistress Katharine, the widow, with her children, gave thanks to the Lord, who had visited them in their affliction. " Thou art a father of the fatherless, and a judge of the widows," faltered the pale lips, " Thou hast not hidden thyself from us, and hast given us beyond what we ask or think."

Help had come from three quarters. The Elector of Saxony, John Frederick the Magnanimous, confirmed Luther's Will, written in the year 1542, and made his family a gift of the 2,000 florins, which were invested for the children in the estate of Wachsdorf.

On the following day, a letter came from the counts of Mansfield, bringing a further gift of 2,000 florins, which was to be put at interest for 100 florins annually.

And lastly, the king of Denmark, Christian III., sent 50 ducts, with the promise that the pension, which Luther with two other theologians of Wittenberg, had during the last years of his life, received from him, should be continued to his widow.

Here was help indeed,—not much among so many, it is true,—but in Luther's school, Katharine had learned contentment, gratitude toward the Ruler of hearts, and trust in the divine Helper.

As a further evidence of God's mercy, men well-known for their honor and integrity, offered themselves as guardians for herself and her children. The captain Asmus Spiegel, and her brother, Hans von Bora, were to act as her advisers, while the care of the children's interests was given over to the Burgo-master, Ambrose Reuter, the Electors' court-physician, Melchior Ratzenberger, and Luther's own brother, Jacob. The Professors Melanchthon and Cruciger offered themselves as additional guardians, to see to it, that their beloved Doctor's children were brought up in the fear of God and in the true doctrine.

The oldest, John, now a youth of twenty, wished to continue his studies, which was granted him. The two younger ones, Paul and Martin, were left in their mother's care ; their tutor, Ambrose Rudtfeld, having proved himself a competent and conscientious teacher,

he was retained.   Gretchen, eleven years old, natu-
rally remained with her mother.

The widow's trust in God was not deceived.   Her
means were scant, it is true.   But Katharine had not
in vain spent twenty years under the influence of her
husband's noble nature.   The lessons she had learned
now proved their value,—and she reaped the interest
upon her spiritual capital.

But it is written :   " How unsearchable are His
judgments, and his ways past finding out."   Thou art
a God that hideth Himself, and wonderful are Thy
dealings with men !   Katharine's trials were not yet
ended, and her tortured heart must needs pass through
the purifying fires of further sorrow.

CHAPTER XXVI.

WAR.

" Evil times are at hand," Luther often said, and the great man had scarcely closed his eyes, when the storm burst.

It had long been evident to discerning eyes, that the Emperor Charles V was only seeking a convenient pretext, for destroying with the sword the fruits of Luther's labors. Realizing their danger, the protestant princes and Cities had formed the Union of Smalcald, and their defensive measures stirred the Emperor's wrath to a still fiercer glow. He was playing a double game ; false alike toward the Protestants and the Pope, he sought merely to strengthen his own power in an Empire, to whose very language he was a stranger.

Having, by means of specious promises, gained the Pope for his purposes, he sought aid in Germany itself for the war of extermination. The Duke of Bavaria was speedily won by the promise of the Elector's hat. Other, smaller potentates, were lured with smaller bribes. Even in the camp of the Protestant prin-

(249)

ces, to their shame be it said, the Emperor found allies; Hans, Margrave of Küstrin, and Eric, Duke
of Brunswick-Calenburg, were not ashamed to wear the
Imperial colors.   Not content with these acquisitions,
the Emperor coveted the alliance of the young and
ambitious Duke Moritz of Saxony, to gain whose good
will, he encouraged the quarrel between the young
Duke and his cousin, the Elector John Frederick of
Saxony.   For the Judas-reward of the Saxon electorate, Duke Moritz betrayed the Protestant faith.

Having secured these confederates, the Emperor
openly continued his preparations.   To the questions of the allies as to his intentions, he scornfully replied : That his purpose was to chastise certain unruly
German princes, who, under the guise of religion, cast
contempt upon the imperial majesty.

It became necessary therefore, to devise a plan, by
which the chastisement designed for themselves, might
rather fall upon the Emperor's back.

The affairs of the Protestants wore a promising as-
pect.   In Upper Germany an army of 47,000 men was
speedily organized under the valiant general Schärtlin,
and it would have been an easy matter to capture the
Emperor, who with 9,000 men lay before Ratisbon.
Schärtlin urged immediate action; but an ill-timed
sentiment of delicacy, which forbade the allies to en-

ter the territory of the neutral Duke of Bavaria, caused
them to hesitate. Their indecision gave the Emperor
time to reinforce his army, and courage, to put the
Elector of Saxony and the Landgrave of Hesse under
the ban of the Empire.

Uniting their forces with those under Schärtlin, the
two outlawed princes advanced upon the imperial army. Much had been lost, but the Emperor might
still have succumbed to the superior strength of the
Protestants. Again their hesitation and indecision
came to his aid. Winter set in. Moritz had gained
time to occupy the Saxon territory and to instal himself as the new sovereign. There was nothing left for
the ex-elector, but to return in haste and re-conquer
his electorate. Schärtlin's army ran short of provisions. The free cities, losing courage, submitted, one
by one, to the Emperor, who in the beginning of 1547
found himself master of the whole of Southern Germany. Shortly after, the Rhenish provinces were lost to
Protestantism.

Then the tide turned.

There was great rejoicing in the Saxon land. The
streets were thronged with people. Cannon thundered
from the ramparts ; bells rang ; flags streamed from the
church-towers ; an eager enthusiasm spread from village
to village, from town to town. The elector, outlawed by

the Emperor, robbed of his sovereignty, had returned to his devoted subjects. Their love was his triumphal chariot, his sword and buckler, the banner under which he not only recovered his own inheritance, but conquered a goodly portion of his ambitious cousin's territory. John Frederick of Saxony, whose destruction had been planned, rose to a higher pinnacle of power than he had ever before occupied. The Emperor trembled with fear and anxiety, and the knowledge that his infamous transaction with Duke Moritz stood revealed before the eyes of all Germany, broke the last remnant of his courage.

He considered his cause well-nigh lost, and despair seized upon his mind. Already it was rumored, that the Bohemians had joined the Elector ! If this were true, then all hope was at an end. Fortunately for him, however, and unfortunately for the Elector, the Bohemians maintained an inexplicable inactivity, allowing their advantages to slip from their grasp, and suffering the Imperial troops to escape from Bohemia, and to follow in the wake of the Elector, who, with an army of 9,000 men, was encamped at Mühlberg on the Elbe ; fearing no evil, and deeming the burning of the Elbe bridge a sufficient security against surprises.

But the burning of bridges was of little use, when treachery guided the enemy to a ford, which made a bridge unnecessary. The name of the miller Strauch is for all time branded with infamy. Out of revenge for the loss of his horses, which the Saxon troopers had carried off, he betrayed his sovereign and his country.

It was a still, peaceful morning, on the Sunday *Quasimodo geniti*, April 24th, 1547. The good elector was sitting in church, devoutly listening to the preaching of the Gospel, when suddenly the noise of a wild tumult broke in upon his devotions. It was the enemy !

The soldiers ran hither and thither, in utter confusion. The officers' commands were unheeded; they all fled wildly toward the heath of Lochau. The elector succeeded in rallying a few of the panic-stricken cavalry regiments, to cover their retreat. But no valor was able to withstand the enemy's superior forces. The Saxon army was cut to pieces and scattered; and the Elector, heroically defending himself, was disabled by a sabre-cut in his face. A look of despair came into his eyes, as he surrendered.

Suddenly a loud thunder-clap was heard, startling all by its unseasonable and unexpected occurrence. But into the Elector's face there came a new light, and with a loud voice he exclaimed: "Yes, Thou mighty God, Thou makest Thyself to be heard. Thou still livest and doest all things well."

Dragged by the Hungarian horsemen into the Emperor's presence, he was received with a look of mingled joy, anger and contempt. The Elector John Frederick Saxony was a prisoner in the hands of the man who had threatened to destroy Protestantism, root and branch; and his electorate was irretrievably lost to him and his race.

.   .   .   .

Wittenberg was in dire confusion. The Emperor was coming, preceded by the rumor that the city of the arch-heretic was to be made to feel the full weight of his displeasure; and was to disappear from the face of the earth, as unworthy of being shone upon by the sun.

The citizens, and among them the widow of the "arch-heretic," prepared to fly. In December of the past year she had been obliged to seek an asylum in Magdeburg, when Duke Moritz advanced upon Wittenberg, and besieged the citadel. But the Elector had hastened to the relief of the city, and recalled the fugitives. Now she must once more bid farewell to her home,—perhaps never to return, for between the Elector's captivity and the Emperor's threat, Wittenberg had small hope of escaping.

Their flight was attended with many hindrances and difficulties. In the general disorder, each one was concerned only for his own safety.· After much persuasion, a teamster was found willing to give the widow and her children a place upon his cart.

He drove in mad haste over the rough roads, belaboring the poor animals with furious blows, and urging them forward, as though the enemy were already at his heels. For hours the wild chase lasted, and night was at hand. The road was uphill, rough and stony; and suddenly the exhausted horses refused to proceed. The teamster, beside himself with rage and fear, forced them on with more blows, when one of the horses, uttering a short, piteous cry, dropped dead. Then he fell to berating the poor beasts, the Emperor, and finally his passengers, whose weight, he asserted, had overtaxed the horses' strength.

Without a word, Katharine and her children climbed down from the cart, and the teamster went on his way.

The widow stood under the open sky; beside her a large chest, containing her most necessary possessions. Not a human being was to be seen near and far. The sky was hung with heavy clouds, and a soft rain was beginning to fall. It was impossible to spend the night in the open air.

For a moment Katharine hesitated; then she beckoned to her sons. They broke open the chest; she

gave to each one as much as he could carry, and com-
forting the frightened children, she said: "Let us go
in God's name! We are everywhere in His keeping;
He will not forsake us!"

They walked rapidly, and half an hour later, a light
shining through the darkness, showed them the way to
the habitations of men. They soon reached a village,
and the first door at which they knocked, was hospita-
bly opened to receive them.

"Good Heavens, Mistress Luther, is it you?" exclaimed a voice from a corner of the dimly-lighted
room, as they entered.

"Master Philip," cried Katharine and the children,
equally surprised. It was Philip Melanchthon, her
husband's dearest friend, whom a similar accident,—
his wagon having been overturned in a ditch—had
driven to seek shelter in the village.

The kind peasants, to whom these exclamations betrayed the identity of their guests, could not sufficiently express their reverent affection. The contents of
the larder were produced for their refreshment. The
beds of the family, in spite of all their protestations,
were given up to the strangers, and on the following
morning, before sunrise, the peasant was at the door,
with his own cart, prepared to carry them to their
journey's end.

"The Lord's chancery," said Melanchthon, as they entered Magdeburg, through the gloomy gate of the fortress. "Your dear husband often gave the city that name. Who would then have thought, that we should one day come hither, to seek safety from persecution. But I thank God, that in these troublous times, he has provided for us a place of refuge."

Katharine found in Magdeburg a number of her friends and acquaintances from Wittenberg, among others the professor of theology, George Major, a dear friend of her departed husband. It was to him she now chiefly looked for protection, as Melanchthon, having upon his hands the care of many other fugitives, was very much engaged.

Here too, the people, for Luther's sake, received his wife and children with open arms. A Senator, in whose house they lodged, made every effort to keep his guests with him permanently. With touching kindness, he and his wife urged Katharine to regard their roomy house as the home of herself and her children ; and, not knowing whether she would ever be able to return to Wittenberg, she finally yielded to their pleading. But she had scarcely consented, when the dreadful tidings were brought them, that the Emperor threatened to put the city under the ban of the Empire, for harboring the Wittenberg fugitives ; and the hearts,

17 ´

which had bounded with renewed hopefulness, sank back again into deeper gloom.

Katharine passed the night in sleepless anxiety, struggling for light. Whither should she go? Was there not, in God's wide world, a spot where the widow of the German Reformer might lay her head?

Early in the morning, she sought Professor Major, whom she found in deep dejection.

"My dear Professor," said Katharine, offering her hand, "it is clear, that we cannot continue in Magdeburg. A plan came to me during the night, and I would ask your assistance in carrying it out."

"Alas, yes," Major interrupted; "we must leave this hospitable place, and our kind friends."

"Hear me," continued Katharine. "We will never find peace within the territories of the Emperor Charles. His threats will ever follow at our heels. Therefore, I think it were best for us, to go whither his arm cannot reach us."

"What do you mean, Mistress Luther?" asked the professor, with wide-open, startled eyes.

"It is a long distance which I propose to travel," said Katharine; "but I do not shrink from it, and the end will reward our labor. I desire to go to Denmark, where under the rule of King Christian the gospel is preached without hindrance. I will go to the champion of the Protestant Confession. He has kept faith with Dr. Martin, and I feel sure that he will take pity on his widow.''

The professor listened, with growing astonishment, and when she had finished, said : '' I approve of your plan, dear Mistress Luther, and wish you a happy journey.''

With a somewhat embarrassed smile, Katharine looked at him. ''But I have a request to add,—a helpless woman cannot alone undertake so arduous a journey, and I would pray you to make this further sacrifice, and accompany me.''

For a moment the professor hesitated, then cheerfully replied : '' It shall be as you wish, dear Mistress Luther.''

On the following morning a wagon, covered with sail-cloth, stood at the Senator's door, to carry away his guests.

The journey proceeded safely, until they reached Brunswick. Here they were detained by the friendliness and solicitude of the Senate of the city, who endeavored to dissuade Katharine from her purpose, and to comfort her with the hope of better times. But she was resolved, and merely urged to greater haste. From Brunswick they travelled in a hired wagon. On the way they encountered frequent troops of lansquenets, and the professor's face grew serious, when he observed the imperial colors. Katharine was alarmed, and begged the driver to hurry toward the village of Gifhorn, visible in the distance. But as they neared the village, the troops became more numerous, and the place itself was thronged with soldiers and camp-followers, so that the travellers were scarcely able to advance. It was still more difficult to find a lodging, in spite of the professor's untiring efforts. The end of their journey, which had seemed so near, was lost in the distance,—vague and unattainable. After a bitter struggle, Katharine abandoned her cherished hope, and on the evening of this day said to her protector: "I cannot endure that you should have so much toil and trouble in my behalf. Let us turn back; it is too dangerous, and I fear that it will be impossible to reach Denmark."

Professor Major nodded sadly; "I do it willingly, for God's sake, yet I think it is His will, that we turn back."

And so they did, the next morning, not knowing whither to go.

Toward noon they halted at an inn, to buy food. In the guest's room sat an elderly man, with a piece of bread and cheese before him. From his appearance, they recognized him as a travelling merchant.

After the customary greetings, it was discovered that he came from Torgau, and was able to give them tidings of Wittenberg.

"The city fared better than any dared hope," he related, "after the reports which preceded the Emperor, that the 'hotbed of heresy' would be made to feel the full measure of his vengeance. But he dealt with it in a merciful and truly royal manner. He had been a traitor, had he done otherwise; for a promise must needs be kept, especially an Emperor's promise."

"What do you mean?" asked the professor.

"Are you perhaps acquainted with Lucas Kranach, the Elector's court-painter?" continued the other.

"How should we not know him?" exclaimed both his hearers.

"It was he who saved the city. He went to the Imperial headquarters, and forcing his way past the guards, walked boldly to the Emperor's tent. Then in all humility, yet confidently, he reminded his Majesty of a promise, he had once made to the painter. I cannot tell, what it was, but the result was, that the Emperor dealt beyond expectation gently with the city of Wittenberg."

"I understand," cried the professor. "Kranach once related to me, how, many years ago, he had met the present Emperor Charles V., when he was still a

boy. If I am not mistaken, Kranach was sent by the
Elector Frederick the Wise as ambassador to Mechlin
in the Low Countries, where the Emperor Maximilian
was at that time holding his court. On this occasion,
the Emperor caused his portrait to be painted by the
distinguished artist ; and the young Prince Charles,
already destined to wear the Imperial Crown of Germany, also desired to sit for his picture. He made
many promises to Master Kranach, that he would be
patient and sit still. But the unruly boy gave the artist much trouble by his restlessness. Yet the portrait
succeeded admirably, and in his childish delight,
pressing Kranach's hands, the prince said to him :
' Master Lucas, when I am a sovereign like my uncle,
and you have a favor to ask of me, it shall be granted.
Here is my hand upon it ! ' And now, it seems, after
so many years, he was able to claim his promise of
the Emperor. Kranach is a noble man,—for himself
he asks nothing, only for others. Herein he resembles him, who counted him among his friends,—the
blessed Dr. Martin !"

Deeply moved, the merchant dried his eyes. " Yes,
he is truly a great and noble man, who thus forgets
himself. I have been further told, that the Emperor
received him very graciously, and made him the most
brilliant offers, if he would enter the imperial service

as court-painter. But Kranach gratefully declined his proposals, requesting instead, that his Majesty deal generously with his captive sovereign, John Frederick of Saxony, as befitted the victor. Kranach said that as he had received many kindnesses and benefits from his gracious master, he therefore would fain show his gratitude, and do what in him lay to ease the prisoner's hard lot."

Katharine listened with brimming eyes; the professor was deeply touched, and a long silence followed the merchant's tale. Then Katharine, turning to him, said: "The city was indeed spared; but a further care presses upon me. I would know the fate of,—" She did not finish the sentence,—her eyes anxiously questioned the merchant's face.

"Be comforted, dear Mistress Luther," he replied. "The Duke of Alva, with his face of parchment and his heart of stone, vehemently urged the Emperor, to have the 'arch-heretic's' ashes scattered to the winds. But his Majesty angrily replied: 'I make war upon the living, not upon the dead.' He even forbade his soldiers to disturb the Lutheran worship. Bugenhagen preached the gospel unhindered, in the presence of many Spanish soldiers; and one day he even observed the Emperor himself among his hearers."

Katharine breathed a sigh of relief, and warmly

thanked the bearer of such good tidings.

Three days later, a woman with her four children knelt at Luther's grave in the Castle-church at Wittenberg, and with many tears, gave thanks that this sacred spot remained undesecrated. It was her first errand,—afterwards she returned to her home in the Augustinian convent.

A dreary sight here met her eyes. The Emperor's orders had not extended to Luther's dwelling, and the spot where the "arch-heretic" had lived, became the scene of savage destruction, and of the brutal revenge of the Spanish soldiery. The household furniture was broken, the cellars robbed of their contents, and the walls soiled with foul doggerel. The children lamented, but Katharine, silently, went about to establish a new home upon the ruins of the old.

CHAPTER XXVII.

MORE TROUBLE.

GREAT courage and a high degree of trust in God were needed, to face the future. The ruined house might have been repaired, but whichever way the widow turned, she saw only desolation.

"Lord, how long!" sighed the poor woman; but the answer was: Thine hour is not yet come; thou shalt enter still further into the dark valley, but my rod and my staff shall comfort thee.

The war had laid waste a large district. The burdens lay heavily upon the drained and ravaged land. Wearily the peasant ploughed his fields, knowing that others would reap the fruit of his toil. With sorrow, Katharine's thoughts reverted to her beloved Zulsdorf, and the fond hopes she had cherished there. But her dear husband had found another resting-place. She had not been permitted, in the peaceful quiet of Zulsdorf, to comfort his declining years with her loving care. And now, in her widowhood, the care of her children's education made a residence there impossible. She had resigned this wish, but hoped to find in her

(265)

farm a means of support.   In consequence of the war,
however, the land had become worthless, and what the
horses' hoofs had spared, was claimed by the sovereign
for the expenses of the war.   Instead of receiving
from Zulsdorf, she was obliged to give.   And Wachsdorf!   She repented bitterly of having urged the purchase of the second estate.   The Chancellor Brück,
had been right in opposing her !

Again, Melanchthon proved himself a trusty friend
and adviser.   He petitioned the Elector Moritz to
remit her share of the war-taxes, and even accompanied her to Leipsic, to the imperial headquarters, to
make her request in person ; but all was of no avail.

On all sides, Katharine saw only broken supports.
The capital secured for her in Mansfeld yielded no
interest ; the war had impoverished her friends there,
and robbed them of the means of keeping their promise. In Torgau, another sat upon the electoral throne,
—a new king had arisen over Egypt, which knew
not Joseph; John Frederick, the kind, generous
prince, in 'whom she had placed her hopes, lay in
chains, and the Emperor held the pen, which was to
sign his death-warrant.

One hope was left,—the king of the Danes, who
had on a former occasion proved a friend in need.
The widow had been prevented from placing her-

self personally under his protection, but the ever-
ready Melanchthon offered to make an appeal in her
behalf to the royal heart.   In his petition he pictured
in moving words the condition of Luther's widow.
Then she waited and hoped, seeing in every stranger
that came to her door a possible messenger from the
king.   But she waited in vain.   Had the letter miscarried? or was the king's heart hardened?

Cruel want knocked at Katharine's door, whither
in former times so many had come, seeking and finding help and comfort.   The world is forgetful, and
returns benefactions with ingratitude.   Katharine had
faithful friends, but they, too, were poor.

Bugenhagen learned to his surprise, that the King
of Denmark had made no reply to Melanchthon's
petition, and, without telling the widow of his purpose, he again pleaded her cause.   But he too hoped
and waited for that which never came.

In the meantime, Katharine made a last effort.
John, her eldest son, was wasting his time at home,
forgetting all that he had learned.   By selling the
greater part of her remaining trinkets and silverware,
she succeeded in raising a few hundred florins.   With
this money, she repaired the one wing of her house,
and took lodgers.   God in his goodness directed the
hearts of some of these, to have compassion with the

widow, and to pay her above what she asked.

One day she led John into her chamber, and falling upon her knees, committed her son to the Lord's keeping.

Early the next morning, the youth set out upon his journey. His mother had filled his knapsack with provisions, and had given him a few of her hard-earned gold-pieces upon the way. Thus supplied, he walked to Konigsberg, where he entered his name as a student of the University.

His mother's blessing followed him, and gave him strength and courage for his work. And her prayer, that the hearts of men might turn in kindness to her son, found a gracious hearing. John entered the service of the Saxon, and afterwards of the Prussian government, and lived to do credit to his father's name.

Katharine was relieved of one pressing care. John's letters from Konigsberg brought good and cheering news. The other children also gave her much pleasure, and it seemed as though a brighter day were about to dawn.

But a fresh trial awaited her: the busy, never-resting hands were forced to be idle,—a slow fever threw her upon a bed of sickness. The physician was puzzled,—he thought the disorder was of the mind, rather than of the body. It became necessary to procure a servant, if the lodgers were to be retained. A maid-servant was hired, to wait upon her, but the discovery of her hypocrisy and dishonesty, added new misery to Katharine's sufferings.

Then followed days, in which she and her children experienced the bitter pangs of hunger. The friends indeed remained,—Melanchthon, Bugenhagen, Cruciger stood by her with unchanging devotion. But she shrank from burdening with her troubles those who had already done so much. Piece by piece, her small store of silver wandered to the silversmith, painful as it was, to part with these witnesses of her former happiness.

But more urgent grew her need,—more hopeless the outlook into the future.

One day, the widow seated herself at the writing-table. Since the representations of Melanchthon and Bugenhagen had failed to move the Danish king, she resolved herself to make a last appeal, trusting that her own words, coming from her troubled heart, might prove effective. Writing was an unwonted occupation, her eyes were dim with tears, and slowly letter was added to letter. After two hours of painful labor, the petition was finished.

" The grace of God through His only Son, Jesus

Christ, our Saviour, to the most gracious and powerful lord and king!

"I humbly pray your Majesty, favorably to regard this my petition, for the reason that I am a widow, and that my dear husband, Dr, Martin Luther, of blessed memory, faithfully served the Christian religion, and enjoyed the special favor of your Majesty. During the latter part of my dear husband's life, your Majesty kindly granted him a pension of fifty ducats, wherefore I thank your Majesty, and pray to God in your behalf. And, inasmuch as I and my children have no support, and these troublous times cause us much distress, I would petition your Majesty, graciously to continue this assistance; for I am sure that your Majesty has not forgotten the great and toilsome labors of my dear husband. Your Majesty is the only king upon this earth, to whom poor Christians may fly for refuge, and because of the benefactions accorded by your Majesty to Christian pastors, their widows and orphans, God will doubtless grant you especial gifts and blessings, for which I shall earnestly and faithfully pray. May the Almighty God mercifully protect your Majesty, and all your house.

"Your Majesty's humble servant,

"KATHARINE,

"Widow of Dr. Martin Luther.

"*Wittenberg, on the 13th of October, A. D. 1550.*"

" They that sow in tears, shall reap in joy," whispered Katharine, as she folded the letter.

Yes, truly, thus is it written in His Word, which cannot fail. But it is also written : " My time is not yet come," and again, "Be patient in tribulation," and "Wait upon the Lord."

Again, the petition was in vain. Months passed, but they brought no reply.

CHAPTER XXVIII.

GLIMPSES OF SUNSHINE.

IF there is consolation in having companions in misery, then Luther's widow might indeed deem herself consoled.

The Elector John Frederick of Saxony, outlawed and dispossessed of his throne, was still a prisoner in the Emperor's hands. Although absent from his subjects, and no longer their master, he yet governed and influenced his people; and from the captive prince a blessing went forth upon all who kept their faith with the Protestant confession. The example of his noble endurance, his heroism, and humble submission inspired thousands, boldly to confess Christ; while on the other hand the unfaithful and the hard of heart were made to feel the shame of their weakness and time-serving.

Luther once said of his friend Hausman : "What we teach, he lives." Had Luther been alive, he might have applied this saying to the Elector also. A man, who has an electorate to sacrifice for his faith, doubtless finds it more difficult to follow Christ, than one who

(272)

had nothing to lose. And all the more glorious does such an one stand before the world. John Frederick appears as a mighty one in Israel, when we consider his heroic calmness, his childlike submission. There was no hesitation, no halting on both sides; his heart was rooted in God's grace, and whether the Emperor sought to tempt him with fair promises, or threatened him with a fearful doom, he never swerved from the faith. His death-sentence was announced to him, while he sat at a game of chess. He calmly finished the game and then said : "I thought your Imperial Majesty would have dealt more mercifully with me ; but if it cannot be otherwise, I beg that the day of my death be made known to me beforehand. There are matters which I wish to arrange with my wife and children." Death has no terrors for him,—his glance says: "To me to live is Christ, and to die is gain."

The Emperor's awakened conscience caused him to revoke the sentence of death, and he promised the Elector liberty and ample indemnification for the ignominy endured, if he would but acknowledge the "Interim" of Augsburg, that masterpiece of Romish craft and deception which, under the guise of yielding to the demands of the Reformation, tore the heart out of Protestantism. He believed himself sure of his game, not deeming it possible that a man should withstand

18

such a temptation, and sacrifice his throne, his honor, and his liberty to the Word of God ; he himself being quite incapable of such an act. Yet he was impressed, and a flush of shame rose to his face, when he heard the Elector's answer :

"I stand as a poor prisoner before your majesty. I do not deny that I have confessed the truth, and for its sake have lost all that I possessed,—my wife and children, my land and my people,—in short, all that God gave and lent me in this world. I have nothing to call my own, save this poor, captive body,—even it is not in my own power, but in that of your majesty. And standing thus despoiled before the world, I am bidden also to renounce my heavenly inheritance by a recantation, from which may God preserve me. For herein have I placed my highest hopes; and I know, that although for its sake I must yield up life, yet will God give me a better possession hereafter. It would ill befit me, by an iniquitous recantation, to mislead so many thousands. Therefore, most gracious Emperor, having me in your power, your Majesty may deal with me as with a prisoner. I will abide by the truth I have confessed; and, as an example to others, willingly suffer, whatsoever God and your Majesty shall lay upon me."

The Emperor averted his face at these words. The

positions were reversed ; the judge stood condemned by his prisoner, and here found himself face to face with a power, which yields to no earthly force. The Lord knocked at the heart of the Emperor Charles, but it refused to answer. Fresh indignities were heaped upon the unfortunate Elector. The Emperor was not ashamed to drag him in triumph through Germany, and even permitted the Spanish guards to exhibit him for money to the curious multitude.

The prisoner's chief consolations were the Bible and Luther's writings, of which he often said, that they penetrated body and soul, and that when he compared other writings with those of Luther, he found in a single page from the latter, more strength, and spiritual nourishment, and consolation, than in a whole book by another. To strike his tenderest spot, the Emperor deprived him of these treasures. His Court-preacher, Master Christopher Hofman, who had been permitted to accompany him, and preach to him the pure word of God, came one day with tears to bid him farewell—at the Emperor's command.

The Elector remained calm and undaunted. " Even though they have taken my books, yet they cannot tear from my heart the lessons I have learned from them ; and even though you go, dear Hofman, the Lord will remain with me.''

When the Emperor found himself powerless to influence the Elector, he endeavored to persuade his sons to accept the Interim. But they refused to act without their father's sanction. His message to them was, "if God's mercy and their father's love were dear to them, to abide steadfastly by his former answer and declaration; and not to suffer themselves to be intimidated, or turned aside, even though the last remnant of their inheritance were taken from them, and still greater dangers threatened. The Almighty God would not forget them, but would graciously protect and defend them."

Great numbers of the Lutheran clergy, refusing to acknowledge the Interim, were driven into misery,—those of Augsburg with the rest. They refused to leave the city, without the blessing of the princely martyr, who just then happened to be in Augsburg.

John Frederick was deeply moved by their words, and turned away to hide his tears; but he speedily conquered himself, and addressing the men, asked: "And has the Emperor forbidden you the entrance to heaven?"

"No," was the answer.

"Then, my friends," cried the Elector, "do not despair. Be of good cheer,—heaven is ours still; and God will surely show you a place upon this earth,

where you will be permitted to preach his word."
He reached into his wallet. "Here is all that I possess in the world. I wish to give you something on
the way. Share it with your brethren. My God will
provide for me further, I trust."

When his fellow-prisoner, the Duke Ernst of Brunswick–Luneberg, began to despair, John Frederick
comforted him: "Do not distress yourself. Since we
have been worsted in the struggle, let us arm ourselves
with patience, and we shall overcome in the end.
Let us show by our actions, that we despise misfortune, and thus shall we wrest the victory from our
enemy's hand. This is the true manner of taking our
revenge."

A second year of misery was added to the first;
the hope of deliverance grew ever fainter; but John
Frederick continued true to himself,—a hero in the
warfare of faith. Like David of old, the God-fearing
monarch, in the midst of his affliction, sounded his
harp and a psalm rang forth from his prison,—a psalm,
whose notes to this day appeal to each human heart,
bringing strength, and peace, and consolation:

> " As God hath willed, so too will I,[1]
> And naught my trust shall alter,

---

[1] Translated by Miss Mary Welden.

In trial and perplexity.
  O, may I never falter.
    All things that be,
    God certainly
For purpose wise is sending;
    What He hath willed
    Must be fulfilled,
To reach a blessed ending.

" As God hath willed it must abide,
    Self-will would but mislead me:
Forbidden joys I'll cast aside,
    And graciously He'll heed me.
      Howe'er it seem,
      I'll rest in Him;
His grace is with me surely;
      Howe'er it seem,
      I'll rest in Him,
    Whose purpose stands securely.

" As God hath willed, I shall obey,
    In all to Him submitting,
Who can His mighty Will gainsay?
    He doth what is befitting.
      Wisdom, nor wit,
      Can alter it.
Nor sorest grief, nor passion;
      My murmuring
      No change could bring,
His hand my way doth fashion.

" As God hath willed, so I will choose,
　　His promises believing,
　　Obedience never more refuse,
　　　But ever to Him cleaving,
　　　　Cast off my fears :
　　　　All days and years
　　　Are by His law designed.
　　　　In this secure :
　　　　His Word is sure,
　　　I'm to His laws resigned.

" As God hath willed, unchanged shall stay,
　　As well the birds might sorrow !
　　If hope forsake the home to-day,
　　　'Tis to return to-morrow.
　　　　The gifts of God
　　　　Are well bestowed ;
　　　And, if He seem unheeding,
　　　　Still let me say,
　　　　Most thankfully,
　　　Unto my good 'tis leading."

Even as, long years ago, Luther's theses, as if borne
on angel's wings, had flown through the length and
breadth of Germany, thus it was with this song of
the captive prince.   In a wondrous manner, its
strains over-leaped the prison-walls, ringing forth into
the world, for thousands to hear.   People sang it in
the churches ; troubled and stricken souls, praying for
guidance, found in it the help they sought ; and to

the conscience of many an one who had fallen from the faith, it came as a messenger of justice from God.

Luther's widow had fastened a copy of the hymn upon the wall opposite her bed; each morning, it greeted her as a voice from above, and each morning she thanked the Elector anew, who herewith gave her more, than he had ever given her in the days of his prosperity.

Money and bread he no longer had to bestow, yet he remained her benefactor, who, until the day of her death, kept his promise to the widow. The stubborn and unbelieving human heart is so prone, in its trouble, to see no further than the present moment, and to regard its own affliction as exceeding all other. But when the cross bearer learns to look about him, and finds that some are still more heavily burdened, he takes heart, to bear his own trials with a meek and quiet spirit. It sometimes seemed to Katharine, as though her burden were heavier than she could bear, and the world's neglect of the widow of him who had been the benefactor of Christianity, appeared doubly shameful. But when she thought of her beloved sovereign, of his heroic endurance, his humble resignation, her cross lost half its weight, and with a blush of shame, she asked forgiveness of God for her faint-heartedness.

This was a glimmer of light in the night of her sorrow, and now at last, a star arose upon her horizon, bringing her a heavenly greeting.

It was on New Year's Day in the year 1552. Katharine has just received the congratulations of her children, when Bugenhagen entered, and from the depths of his kind, faithful heart, spoke to the widow words of comfort and encouragement.

When Katharine had expressed her own hearty good wishes for his welfare during the coming year, Bugenhagen continued : " I greatly wondered, for what cause the King of Denmark made no reply to our repeated petitions in your behalf, knowing as I do, his kind and merciful heart, and he having regularly transmitted to Melanchthon and myself our usual pension. Yesterday a young man came to me, who has travelled much, and was employed as Secretary at the Danish Court, whither he is shortly to return. When I expressed to him my surprise that the king had thus withdrawn his accustomed aid, he was much astonished, and could not otherwise explain the matter, than that the letters must have miscarried ; for, as he said, the conversation one day turned upon the widow of Dr. Luther, when one of the royal officers said that no doubt she was in comfortable circumstances, as she had not petitioned his majesty for a con-

tinuance of the pension. Herefrom, dear Mistress
Luther, you perceive that the king knows nothing of
your need. I would therefore advise you to venture
another letter, which I will entrust to the secretary,
when he leaves, and I trust that it will not prove
fruitless."

Katharine thanked her friend, and did as he advised. When she learned that the young man pur-
posed to set out upon his journey on the 9th of January, she sat down and wrote :

" Most gracious lord ! Accept my humble service
and my feeble prayers to God in your majesty's
behalf.

Your majesty doubtless remembers, that my dear
husband, of blessed memory, also Master Philip
Melanchthon and Dr. Bugenhagen received annually from your majesty a pension, toward the support of their families; which has heretofore been
regularly paid out to Dr. Pommer and Master Philip. And inasmuch as my dear husband was well-
inclined to your majesty, regarding you as a most
Christian king, and as your majesty at all times greatly
favored my husband—for which I am humbly grateful—I feel myself constrained, by reason of my great
need, to petition your majesty, hoping that you will
pardon this request of a poor widow. I would pray,

that this money be continued to me. Your majesty doubtless knows how, since my husband's death, war and trouble have visited our land ; how the poor have been oppressed, and how many have been made widows and orphans, so that one cannot but feel pity, all of which were too long to relate. For these and other reasons, I am forced to make this appeal, trusting that your majesty will kindly grant my petition, and receive the reward of the Almighty God, who is the friend of widows and orphans. Into the keeping of that same God, the Father of our Lord Jesus Christ, I commend your majesty, praying that He may grant you long life for the sake of His Church, and graciously keep and preserve you from all danger to body or soul. Amen.''

''Your Majesty's humble servant,

''KATHARINE LUTHER,

'' Dr. Martin's Widow.

'' *On the 8th of January, in the year 1552.*''

When Katharine gave the letter to Dr. Bugenhagen to read, he added these few words : '' Father Luther's widow is in sore straits, and therefore petitions your majesty for relief, having, together with her neighbors, suffered great losses during the year.''

On the following day the secretary left, carrying the

letter with him, which he delivered into the king's own hands.

Once more, Katharine was obliged to take from the corner cupboard three silver cups, and to carry them to the silver-smith, but she went with a lighter heart, feeling that help was near.

She was not deceived, for sooner than she dared to hope, on the 20th of March, a messenger from the King of Denmark brought her fifty ducats, with the king's greeting.

Here was another glimpse of sunshine in the dreary life of her widowhood, and a renewed assurance that the God of our fathers still lived. His faithfulness and mercy had even better things in store for her,—his angel was already upon the way—bringing His message to the sufferer : " Blessed are they that mourn, for they shall be comforted."

CHAPTER XXIX.

RELEASE.

THE situation of Wittenberg was not a healthy one. The vapors arising from the broad flats of the Elbe were doubtless favorable to the growth of vegetation, —but scarcely to the health of human beings. The moat surrounding the walls, and half-filled with stagnant water, contributed its share to the noisome odors which poisoned the air. Several times during Luther's lifetime the plague, beside other epidemics, had made fearful havoc among the citizens; it returned again in the summer of 1552, and raged with renewed fury.

The angel of death was followed as usual, by his most powerful ally,—fear. Men had learned no lessons from experience, or they would have remembered that a calm temper is the most effective safe-guard against the pestilence; and again, death reaped an abundant harvest. In the universal distress, charity was dead, and selfishness stood revealed in its most hideous form. Children forsook their dying parents; the gravediggers left the neglected corpses lying by

(285)

the wayside : superstition, with its senseless remedies helped many an one to his death, while others with fiendish malice carried the seeds of the pestilence into uninfected houses.

Many of the citizens sought safety in flight.   The University was closed at the Elector's command, professors and students repairing to Torgau.

Katharine had learned from her husband, calmly to commit herself to the Lord's care, and to help, wherever she was able.   The opportunity was thus given her, of heaping coals of fire upon the heads of many, who had closed their hearts to her in the time of her need.

For five weeks the plague had raged in Wittenberg, still sparing Katharine's household.   Then one of her lodgers was stricken down, and died.   She had no fear, at least not for herself,—for her desire was, to depart and be with Christ, and with her beloved husband.   Yet she was concerned for her children's sake, and finally resolved to leave Wittenberg, and go to Torgau.

As usual, she lost no time in carrying out her decision.   A few days later, a large, canvas-covered wagon held at the door of the Luther-house, to carry away the widow and her children with their most necessary belongings.

Katharine's eyes rested sadly upon the spot, where she had enjoyed so much happiness during her husband's life, and had experienced so much affliction since his death. The human heart is bound with a thousand cords to its earthly home; and not only the joys of the past, but its sorrows also, exercise a magnetic power, which makes parting a bitter trial.

Katharine was very sad. Hot tears gushed from her eyes, and she stood hesitating at the open gate, until the horses grew impatient and the driver urged her to make haste.

Their road led them through the Elster-gate, and past the garden, whose dense shrubbery recalled so many pleasant hours. Further on, at a little distance from the road, rose the summer-house beside the fountain, where her husband was wont to receive his friends, and where they spent many hours together in earnest labor or in cheerful talk. It seemed to her like taking leave of her life, as one by one, the scenes of her departed happiness vanished from her sight.

She sat lost in melancholy revery, and the children, divining her thoughts, feared to disturb her, or to relieve the heaviness of their own hearts. Only the driver was insensible to their grief, and swore lustily at his horses, who refused to settle to a quiet pace.

Katharine roused herself at last, and saw to her dismay that the horses were being controlled with difficulty. As they passed through the outskirts of a village, a dog ran out and barked at them. This so excited the frightened animals that they became entirely unmanageable. They plunged and dashed furiously down the road.

Katharine was in deadly fear. Scarcely conscious of herself, she suddenly rose from her seat, and sprang from the wagon. She could not have chosen a more unfavorable spot, for by the roadside ran a stream of water, with steep banks. In alighting, she struck against a stone and slipped into the water. With the help of a peasant who hurried to their assistance, the driver succeeded in quieting the horses; Katharine, wet to the skin, and stunned by her fall, was unable to rise; she was lifted into the wagon, and covered with warm wraps.

Two hours later they reached Torgau. Lodgings had been taken for them in a house near the convent church. The landlord, Kasper Grünewald by name, and a worthy man, had been a friend of Luther's. As the Saviour said of Mary Magdalene, it might be said of him: He hath done what he could. It seemed like paying a debt of love to his departed friend, when he could shelter the widow in his house;

and he vied with her children in giving her the tenderest care.

Katharine was at once put to bed ;—the fright and the chill had made her very weak, and brought on a high fever.

The physician who was called in, shook his head, and did all that his skill suggested, to revive the sinking forces. It seemed as though all were concerned in repairing the world's neglect of the widow of the great man.

She appreciated their efforts. Her lips overflowed with gratitude, and when her growing weakness deprived her of the power of speech, her eyes and the mute pressure of her hand conveyed her thanks.

The loveliest roses bloomed upon her cheeks; and her skin was lily-white and transparently pure. She did not seem ill, and never in her life had she been fairer. A strange light shone in her eyes, and her manner was so gentle and tender, that those who entered her presence, seemed to feel a breath from the other world. Her thoughts were in Heaven, more than upon the earth. She often spoke of her husband, not only in her waking moments, but also in her dreams; and sometimes she spoke *to* him, as though he were actually present.

Winter came, with its snow-flakes and its ice-flow-

19

ers, with its long nights, and the holy calm of the Advent Season. "Come, Thou Saviour of the Gentiles,"—they sang in the churches; and in the street, under the sick woman's window, the choir-boys repeated the sacred strains.

She listened to the sweet, joyous tones; her cheeks flushed, her eyes glowed, and she softly sang, "Come, Thou Saviour of the Gentiles." Then she folded her hands, and inspired with sudden strength, she prayed: "Lord, my Saviour, Thou standest at the door, and wouldst enter in. O come, Thou beloved guest, whom my soul awaits with longing. For I desire to depart and to be with Thee. Grant me a peaceful end, and a blessed departure from this valley of tears. Let my poor children be committed to Thy mercy,— that none of them be lost, but that all may one day appear before Thy throne, and unite with us in praising Thy glorious Name. And, Lord, look down in mercy upon Thy Church, which the pope and other ungodly men would fain rend in pieces, extinguishing the light of the Gospel truth which, by Thy servant, the blessed Dr. Martin, Thou didst kindle in our German land. Have mercy upon all, who for the Gospel's sake suffer shame and persecution, and give them strength, boldly to confess their faith, that Thy Name may through them be glorified. I give Thee thanks,

that Thou didst regard the misery of our beloved
Elector, and didst turn his captivity, that men may
see how Thou dost bring to honor those who have
suffered for Thy Name's sake. Grant him a calm and
peaceful old age, and finally take him home to Thee.
Dear Lord, I thank Thee for all the trials, through
which Thou didst lead me, and by which Thou didst
prepare me to behold Thy Glory. Thou hast never
forsaken nor forgotten me ; Thou hast evermore caused
Thou face to shine upon me, when I called upon
Thee. Behold, now I grasp Thy hand and say, as
Jacob of old : Lord, I will not let Thee go, unless
Thou bless me! I will cling to my Lord Jesus
forevermore. Amen. Help me, dear Lord God.
Amen."

She had spoken in a low tone, pausing frequently.
Now she lay exhausted. Her hands were clasped ;
her eyes turned upward, as though she were watching
for the coming of the Lord.

Those around her prayed softly.

The hours passed ; night came. They lighted the
lamp, and kindled a fresh fire in the stove, for it was
a bitter cold day, the 20th of December, in the year
1552.

As it struck nine, the mother turned to her children, whose faces had grown wan and pinched with watching and anxiety. "Had you not better lie down and sleep, my dear children?" she whispered. "I too am tired."

Then, assisted by Gretchen, she turned to the wall, closed her eyes and breathed quietly.

The children sat in silence by her bedside, watching their mother's sleep, and fondly hoping that it might be the sleep of returning health. About an hour passed thus.

Then Margaret rose, and softly creeping to the bed, she leaned over her mother. She listened—all was still: The patient sufferer was at home with her God.

THE END.